ACCELERATION

ACCELERATION

Been hunting. Riding the subway, searching the
faces for the right one. All the pretty ladies
sitting across from me. I'm ...
A cool

GRAHAM McNAMEE

WENDY
LAMB
BOOKS

Published by
Wendy Lamb Books
an imprint of
Random House Children's Books
a division of Random House, Inc.
New York

Wendy Lamb Books is a trademark of Random House, Inc.

Visit us on the Web! www.randomhouse.com/teens
Educators and librarians, for a variety of teaching tools,
visit us at www.randomhouse.com/teachers

Library of Congress Cataloging-in-Publication Data
McNamee, Graham.
Acceleration / Graham McNamee.
p.   cm.
Summary: Stuck working in the Lost and Found of the Toronto
Transit Authority for the summer, seventeen-year-old Duncan finds
the diary of a serial killer and sets out to stop him.
ISBN 0-385-73119-1 (trade)—ISBN 0-385-90144-5 (GLB)
[1. Serial murderers—Fiction.   2. Diaries—Fiction.   3. Summer
employment—Fiction.   4. Toronto (Ont.)—Fiction.   5. Canada—Fiction.
6. Mystery and detective stories.]   I. Title.
PZ7.M232519Ac 2003
[Fic]—dc21
2003003708

Printed in the United States of America

October 2003

10 9 8 7 6 5 4 3 2 1

BVG

For Mom and Dad, thanks for everything.

And thanks to the Canada Council for the Arts for their support.

ACCELERATION

ONE

This is a nightmare.

Working at the Toronto Transit Commission's lost and found. Nine to five. Monday to Friday. A little slice of death, one day at a time.

For me it's a two-month sentence, July and August. I would have been happy bumming around till September, but Dad called in a favor to get me in here. And at least I don't have to wear a uniform like my bud Wayne over at the Dairy Barn. Wayne's planning to torch the thing on Labor Day (the uniform, not the Barn) before we head back for our last year of high school.

So I'm here under protest, a political prisoner of the capitalist overlord otherwise known as Dad.

Here's the one-minute tour of the place. First, to get here you have to come to Bay subway station and take the service elevator down to the subbasement. At the end of the hall to your left you'll find the door marked LOST AND FOUND. Jacob, my supervisor, sits at the front counter cataloguing the lost junk that comes in from the buses and subways in the transit system. If you think of a half-deflated soccer ball with two of the hairiest ears you've ever seen attached to it, you've got a good picture of Jacob. Past the counter there's a maze of stacks holding row after row, shelf after dusty shelf of lost stuff.

I'm trying on a black leather jacket in the stacks when the bell at the counter dings. The jacket's term expires in a week, so it'll soon be appearing in my closet as part of the Duncan collection. One ding of the bell means Jacob needs me to search for something. Two dings means hurry up. Three dings—things get ugly.

When I get to the counter, Jacob's asking an old woman about the weather up on the surface. Spending eight hours a day in this dungeon, you tend to forget that the sun is still shining up there.

"They say it's going to hit a hundred and three today," the woman tells him. "Not a cloud in the sky."

It's been six weeks with no rain. Major heat wave. But down here you'd never know. The city could be bombed to ashes and we'd still be here sorting through the piles.

"Duncan, we're looking for a pair of glasses," Jacob tells me. "Silver frames. Bifocals."

I sigh. "Right. This might take a while."

Eyeglasses rank in the top four on the list of most often lost items, right up there with umbrellas, cell phones, and books.

I'm the runner, the one who does the actual searching. Jacob does the actual *sitting*.

I don't know who did this job before me—don't know if

anybody did it before me—but the place is a mess. The way it works, stuff gets held here for three months. Everything's got a Post-it with an expiration date. Anything unclaimed gets boxed up for the quarterly sale down at the YMCA. But if you poke around, you'll find stuff that's been here for two years or more. I pulled a college sweater off the top shelf the other day, and the dust coming off it drifted down like snow.

Lost junk is organized in sections. All the jackets are together, including my black leather beauty. Dozens of umbrellas are heaped in a pile, enough rain protection to keep every last flea on Noah's ark dry. There's a library of forgotten books overflowing the packed shelves. And there are two boxes of eyeglasses, separated into sunglasses and regular. I dig in.

There's an amazing variety, everything from prescription swimming goggles to your basic thick-black-framed geek glasses to your old-lady specials with the necklace holders attached to the arms. I find a pair that fits the lady's description—bifocals, silver frames. Holding them up to peer through the lenses, I see they've got enough magnifying power to count the hairs on a mosquito's butt.

"That's them," the old woman says after trying them on.

Jacob makes her sign the claims book, as if the glasses are worth more than the dollar they'd get at the Y sale.

"I'm lost without these," she tells us. "I'm so blind without them, I didn't realize until I was halfway here that I'd put hand lotion on my face instead of sunscreen. I can already feel a burn starting up."

Jacob nods. "Yeah. With the holes in the ozone and global warming, the sun's not as friendly as it used to be."

The woman shivers, pulling her jacket closed. "Well, it's certainly cool down here."

"We're about fifty feet underground—deeper than the subway tunnels—so the temperature stays a constant cool year-round. This must be what it feels like to be buried alive." That's Jacob's idea of funny. I think he's been down here too long.

The woman gives him a nervous look and mumbles her thanks as she makes for the door.

"You've really got a way with the ladies," I say when she's gone.

No response.

I fill a paper cup at the cooler, leaning on it as it gurgles to itself, and watch the clock crawl toward eternity. Jacob goes back to reading the newspaper.

Past him, there's a glass case on the wall that once held a fire axe but now has an artificial leg standing inside. That leg is like the official mascot of all the forgotten junk in the lost and found. There's a worn-down blue men's Puma running shoe on its foot, and it's obviously been well used. It always gets me wondering—how do you lose something like that? I mean, didn't the guy notice something was missing when he went hopping off the subway—that the world was bouncing up and down more than usual? What happened, that he never came back to claim it? Jacob says the thing's been here for three years.

He taps his pen on the counter, pondering the word jumble in today's *Lifestyle* section. He taps the seconds away, tapping seconds into hours into days. Jacob's a lifer. He doesn't even hear the clock anymore.

I'm going stir-crazy down here. I mean, look at Jacob with his hairy gray ears; wrinkles creasing into other wrinkles until his face looks like he fell asleep on a screen door. Then there's the wet clicking sound he makes when he's playing with the upper plate of his false teeth. Two months down here and that's what I'm going to look like.

I push off from the cooler and wander back into the stacks to kill the last half hour of the day. Subway thunder rumbles through the ceiling as a train pulls into Bay Station. A slight draft breezes through the room whenever a train goes by, and the fluorescent lights overhead flicker at the rumbling, like torches in the wind. It feels like a medieval dungeon down here.

I have a lawn chair set up back in the stacks for when I get tired of staring at Jacob and he gets tired of me bitching. Nearby are the shelves of lost books. Old and new. Hardcover, paperback, science fiction, romance, mystery, medical, true crime, horror, history—anything and everything.

Scanning the titles, I see a few Stephen Kings I've already read.

And then there's a small, thick hardcover. No jacket, no title on the spine. Just plain brown leather. I sit back on my lawn chair and flip through it.

Not really a *book* book at all, it's some kind of journal or notebook. I turn the yellow-edged pages. Near the beginning I find what looks like notes from a science experiment. There's a graph showing different times running vertically up the side, with different liquids listed horizontally along the bottom. At first I think it's a graph of how long each liquid takes to reach the boiling point. We did that one in chemistry a few years ago.

It's hard to tell. This person's handwriting is like epileptic chicken scratch. Filling the margins are doodles in black and green ink of all different kinds of eyes. Round eyes, slit eyes, bloodshot and crying eyes, and ones that look like they've come loose from their sockets. Real seventh-grade gross-out stuff.

It takes me a couple seconds to crack the code and decipher what the caption says at the top. DROWNING TIMES. It's underlined twice in green. I focus on the crabbed writing at the bottom of the page.

white mice. litter of six. ten weeks old.

I study the graph again. On the side are times ranging from zero to five minutes. Along the bottom different liquids are listed: *water, turpentine, beer, Windex, gasoline.*

This is no science experiment—at least none we ever did in school.

I look at the various times in relation to liquids, understanding finally what it means. My stomach twists around. It's an experiment to find out how long it takes for mice to drown in different liquids.

This is really warped.

I turn a few more pages and find some yellowed newspaper clippings. One reads:

On March 14, two cats were found hanging by their necks from lengths of chain, nailed to telephone poles in a back alley of Wilson Heights. The animals had been eviscerated. Anyone with information is asked to call Crimestoppers.

The word *eviscerated* is circled in red, and in the margin the writer of this thing has scribbled: *Big word from a small mind.*

There are other clippings, with headlines reading: GRISLY DISCOVERY, ANIMAL ABUSE EPIDEMIC, PET OWNERS WARNED TO KEEP CATS INDOORS.

This is some sick nut's little diary.

I drop the book on the floor, wiping my palms on my jeans, feeling dirty just from touching it. I shake my head. The world is full of ugly, twisted people. There, that's my Mr. Rogers thought for the day.

The bell at the front desk rings five times. Either it's quitting time or Jacob's having a stroke. Getting up, I step on the book like it's a roach I'm trying to kill. Then I kick it so it skitters across the cement floor.

Walking away down the aisle, I can't help thinking how it's not always that easy to kill a roach.

TWO

I had the dream again. It's been a couple of months since the last one. I was hoping I could forget about it, hoping it would forget about me. Leave me alone.

The dream's always the same. When I was little I used to hate reruns on TV, the way everybody would make the same mistakes over again. That's what the dream is, a rerun where everything that went wrong the first time goes wrong again. And no matter how hard I fight I can't change anything.

Here's how it goes.

A blistering day at Kayuga Beach. I'm in the water, about eight feet deep, skimming along the sandy bottom. It's clear enough that I can see the muddy clouds my hands stir up with every stroke.

Mom says I was born to swim. She took me to baby swim classes before I could even walk. She'd hold her hand under my stomach and I'd start paddling like I was ready to do laps. I saw on TV somewhere how it's a natural instinct; comes from evolving from fish. They say when you're real tiny in the womb, for a few weeks there, you have gills.

So that's me. Fishboy.

I used to time how long I could hold my breath underwater. Two minutes thirty seconds I hit one time, turning purple with my lungs exploding.

I'm running out of air now, kicking up to the surface to breathe again. I squint against the million-watt sunlight. Back on the beach I can just make out where Wayne and Vinny are sucking down Slurpees.

There's a girl screaming in the water, probably getting splashed or playing tag. Girls are always screaming—at the beach, in school, on MTV.

I dive under again, where it's quieter. Some sound travels underwater. Like those motorboats out on the lake. They're a mile away, but I can still hear them down here, kind of like a mosquito buzzing. The water's getting deeper, the bottom dark and cool, the sand turning to black mud.

Pearl divers can hold their breath for five minutes, so they can get to the bottom, where the oysters are, and back. I once watched a frog sit underwater for fifteen minutes, just hanging out. No panic. Like it could live down there.

Between one stroke and the next, the temperature drops from cool to near freezing, and the light filtering down disappears. Dark as midnight here. I can't have gone so deep so fast. Pushing off the bottom, my feet sink into the mud a few inches. For a second it's like the mud doesn't want to let me go, and I have to kick to get loose. Swimming to the surface takes longer than it should. It's as if with every stroke I take, the water gets that much deeper, like I'm swimming in place. My lungs start to burn, and there's the growing thunder in my ears of my own heartbeat amplified. I feel like shouting but there's no air left, and nobody to hear.

I break the surface gasping, blinded by the sun after the cold midnight below. Feeling dazed and dizzy, I hear screaming. I'm so disoriented for a second I wonder if it's me.

But no. It's that girl still, her shrieks broken up by coughs and splashing. I turn in the water, dog-paddling. The people back on the beach are so far away they look like insects. And they're all rushing into the lake now, a dozen ants swimming out toward me. But it's not me they're headed for. It's the girl. I try to stretch up and see farther across the surface, above the small waves making their way to shore.

And there, about thirty feet away, between me and the beach, I see an arm flailing, fighting against the water. For maybe a quarter of a second a face is visible above the surface, a pair of eyes. Wide eyes, blind with fear.

I'm frozen for a second by that look. I've never seen anyone so scared. But then my brain clicks and I realize that we're too far out for those people rushing toward us to get here in time.

There's only me. So I kick toward her, my arms flying in a frantic crawl. The water seems to stretch like before, only now it's not getting deeper but wider, dragging her farther away from me like some freak riptide. Between strokes, I catch freeze-frames of her going under, the water churning around her. Her mouth wide open, choking and screaming, fighting for air. Eyes wild, and dark as the black mud at the bottom of the lake. Then there's just an arm sticking up. I'm maybe ten feet away when her hand disappears.

Sucking a deep breath, I go after her into the dark, my arms swinging around like a blind man's, searching for anything—a hand, a foot, a head.

Nothing. I plunge deeper, my eyes wide but useless. The water's so cold it hurts, freezing my muscles into tight cramps. My hands find nothing. And my breath finally gives out.

That's when I wake up in bed, gasping, my heart like a machine gun. The dark of my room is a soft gray, nothing like the dead black of the water. It takes me a few minutes to convince myself I've really escaped the nightmare.

It's the kind of dream that makes you try and stay awake after, because you know it's waiting there for you behind your closed eyelids.

A dream. But not a dream. It happened for real last September. Labor Day weekend at Kayuga Beach, Lake Ontario. The last blast of summer before school. The girl's name was Maya. I didn't know her, but I was the last person to see her alive.

I was the one who didn't save her.

THREE

I need a name. If you don't make one up for yourself, the media slaps one on you. They called David Berkowitz the .44-Caliber Killer, but that was weak. He called himself Son of Sam. Sounds better. Don't know what it means, but it sounds good. The Green River Killer—again, weak. They just named him after his dumping ground. The Zodiac Killer picked his own name, and nobody ever forgot it.

I need a name. It's going to be on everybody's lips. I'm going down in history.

FOUR

"What do you think?" I ask Vinny, showing off my new black leather jacket in his living room.

"Man, how much are they paying you?"

"Not enough. But I got this beauty for free."

"What? You ripped it off?" Vinny says.

"I got it from work," I tell him. "Unclaimed at the lost and found."

"So you ripped it off."

"Please. Unclaimed items go to a sale over at the Y. I just saved it the trip. It's one of the perks of the job. This baby was lost, but now it's found."

I grab a seat on the couch.

Vinny's mom is crazy about colors—he says she's still trying to recover from not getting the sixty-four-piece crayon set in kindergarten—so the color scheme in this apartment is kind of intense. Deep orange walls (Tangerine Gold, she calls it), red furniture (Autumn Burgundy), and yellow carpeting (Amber Sunset). The weird thing is, you get this explosion of hues in here, but the windows are all covered in tinfoil, blocking the wicked afternoon sun. It gives the room a weird, artificial-sunset kind of feel.

"I just got off work," I say. "Come on, let's go grab something at the Dairy Barn."

"You buying?"

"We're going to use our employee discount." Which means our *Wayne* discount, him being the new slave to minimum wage down at that grease pit.

Vinny takes a minute to change from his ratty old sweatshirt into his uniform: jeans, black T-shirt, and an army surplus jacket two sizes too big. Poor guy has no sense of style. He wears the same thing every day, winter or summer, blizzard or blistering. His left hand, which was hidden in the stretched sleeve of his sweatshirt before, is now stuffed in his jacket pocket. He usually keeps it out of sight. Tell you why later.

"It wouldn't kill you to expand your wardrobe a little," I tell him. "You've been wearing that stuff for two years straight."

He shrugs. "So I'm not a slave to fashion."

"I'm going to leave this here," I say, taking off my leather. "It's a beauty, but it makes you sweat like a hog. You got any wooden hangers?"

"What is this, the presidential suite? I've got plastic. Live with it."

We take off. Vinny lives in G building. I'm over in C. That's how they name the buildings in what's known in the neighborhood as the Jungle.

Don't get the wrong idea. It's not like the projects you see on TV, with drive-by shootings, Chihuahua-sized rats, and kids falling down elevator shafts. The Jungle is just a worn-down kind of place where the kids run wild and herds of cats live out back by the garages. It's right on the edge of an industrial wasteland—factories, a steel mill and a strip mall a couple blocks down. Some kids at school call the place Welfare Towers, which is a lie. People here work. Most of them. They're just not rich.

"So what did you do today?" I ask Vinny.

He shrugs, squinting in the white sunlight. "I don't know. I woke up. End of story."

Here's the deal with Vinny.

First time I saw him was playing soccer in gym class, grade eight. He was the new guy in school. It was shirts versus skins, and Vinny was chosen by the skins.

"No way. I'm not taking it off," he told the teacher.

Vinny wasn't just wearing a shirt, though, he had on his jacket too. Like he was too cool for soccer. And he kept his left hand stuffed in the pocket.

"Why not?" Mr. Pitt asked. Then after a second staring Vin down, he just said: "Oh."

I guess Pitt figured out why not by himself, even though it was a mystery to the rest of us. "Okay, you're with the shirts then," he said.

Wayne nudged me with his elbow. "You think he's got a gun in that pocket?" he said.

I had to laugh. Wayne thinks life is a movie.

"Yeah, Wayne. He's been sent from the future to kill you."

It was a cool September afternoon and the leaves were already falling, so me and Wayne weren't real happy to be skins either.

"Hey, I want to be a shirt too," Wayne called out.

"Forget about it," Pitt told him. "You're a skin."

He blew his whistle and we took our end of the field.

"What's with the new meat?" Wayne asked me. "He gets to wear a parka, and I have to freeze my butt off?"

So you see, we had something against Vinny from the start. New guy getting special treatment and all. So maybe we gave him a little extra attention—attention of the tripping and shoving kind. Nothing major, no concussions, just our way of getting his precious jacket dirty.

I was going for the ball when me and Vinny got tangled up, and both of us went crashing to the ground. My head hit the turf and I lay there for a second, trying to figure out which way was up. I watched Vinny push himself to his knees. His left hand was out of his pocket now as he reached to the grass to balance himself. There was something funny about that hand. It took me a second to focus; then I realized what it was. On the end of a skeleton-thin forearm, his left hand only had three fingers. Not even that really— there was a middle, an index and half a thumb. It looked sort of like a claw.

"What's wrong with your hand?" I asked.

He looked me in the eye like I'd just insulted him.

"Nothing," he said, shoving it back in his pocket. "What's wrong with your face?"

Good comeback, I thought.

Later, I told Wayne about the claw hand and the skeleton arm. In school, you can't keep something like that hidden for long. Try going around using only one hand for a day and you'll see what I mean. So everybody was asking what happened to it.

Right off the bat, I'll tell you I'm a nosy guy. I've got these big satellite-dish ears that can pick up a cricket farting at twenty feet. So I heard kids asking him, What's with the hand?

First he said: "It was an accident. I was helping my father—he's a fireworks expert—mix chemical powders for a New Year's Eve show. A lightbulb blew and threw sparks down into the powder. *Boom!* And they never even found the missing fingers."

Second: "I got caught in a drive-by shooting outside an arcade, downtown. I was the only one hit. They said the fingers were too mashed to reattach."

Third—and this was my favorite: "When I was four, I was kidnapped and held for ransom. My family's rich. But when the money didn't come fast enough, the kidnappers cut off one of my fingers for every day the ransom was late. Then they mailed them to my parents."

He'd obviously been explaining his hand for years and

had figured out some juicy lies. The thing is, people believed him. I mean, how could they not? The evidence was right there in front of them.

The truth was boring. Months after we crashed on the soccer field, after I found out he'd moved into the Jungle and we started hanging out, he finally spilled it.

A birth defect had left him with a skinny twisted arm and half a hand. No story. No action.

"I think I like the lies better," I told him.

"Me too," Vinny said. Then a smile spread across his face. "Did I ever tell you how, when I was a baby, a pit bull dragged me from my stroller and chowed down on my fingers? Swallowed them whole."

FIVE

At the Dairy Barn I order a banana split.

"And hold the roaches," I say.

Wayne stares back at me from the other side of the counter. He's wearing the Barn's polyester uniform, stained with a shotgun blast of ketchup on the shoulder and lower-caliber blotches of hot fudge and mustard on the sleeves.

"We don't do special orders," he says.

"Okay, then leave them in."

I pay and go grab a seat with Vinny. As we head into week seven of this heat wave, the sun feels like it's about to go supernova and burn us all to ash. But there Vin sits in his oversized jacket. I get why he wears it, but I still think he's deranged. Vinny yawns, leaning back against the wall and stretching his legs out on his half of the booth.

"What do *you* have to yawn about?" I ask him. "You've been sleeping in since school let out."

"Hey, I still wake up at the crack of noon every day. Anyway, you know how I look up to you guys, slaving away for the Man. Did I ever tell you you're my hero?"

"Yeah, the last time you tried to bum some money off me."

Wayne appears with our splits. That's our employee discount—whatever we order one of, he brings two. We got connections. "Hey, ladies. What's up?"

"I love a man in uniform," says Vinny.

Wayne coughs a laugh. "That's so funny I just forgot which one of these I spit in."

Wayne tosses his Barn cap on the table, grabbing a seat and scratching the new dark fuzz on his usually shaved head. His cap has a grease stain on the front that looks like the state of Florida. Employees are expected to launder their own uniforms, but Wayne wears his stains as a political statement, an act of slobby civil disobedience.

"You're not eating?" I ask him.

He shakes his head. "I can't eat that stuff anymore. Just the smell of it makes me want to chuck."

"You're never going to make employee of the month talking like that," I tell him.

Strange to see how Wayne's gone straight. Back in kindergarten he was voted most likely to do hard time. They use his old finger paintings as psych tests for the criminally insane.

Ever since we were little he's taken me under his evil wing, teaching me the ways of the Dark Side of the Force—Vader to my Luke. He stuffed my first-ever *lifted* CD in my jacket, and told me when to run. He took me on wrecking sprees, trashing construction sites. But he's always been strictly small-time, doing victimless crimes. His biggest heist was boosting half a dozen Discmans from the loading dock at the Wal-Mart.

I've known him forever. He's like family, in a twisted way. We grew up together. Got arrested together. Did community service together. Beat the crap out of each other a couple times. And now we're growing old together, rotting away from nine to five, five days a week. Where did it all go wrong?

I can remember when we had promising careers as juvenile delinquents ahead of us. Until we got caught doing something seriously stupid.

This was how Wayne talked me into it.

"Easy money. Nobody gets hurt. Nobody even owns the stuff really. How could it be stealing if nobody even owns it?"

That was a deep question. His logic wouldn't stand up if you leaned on it, but I was bored and there was nothing else to do.

This was the middle of October, four years ago. It was at the tail end of a teachers' strike, so you couldn't really blame us—we were without guidance.

The development off Black Creek Drive had about a dozen new houses being finished. Not luxury places, but still *castles* compared to our apartments back in the Jungle. And in these castles they had cutting-edge, top-of-the-line toilets.

"Toilets?" I asked Wayne. "We're going to go all the way down there to break in and take a leak?"

He shook his head at me like I was the idiot. "Do you know how much toilets go for?"

I let that question die in silence.

"So you want us to deal hot toilets?" I said, starting to laugh before I saw he was serious.

"Those things go for like six hundred bucks," Wayne told me. "New places like that will have the absolute best. Brand-new designer stuff."

"And what's your master plan for selling them—set up on a corner downtown, 'Wanna buy a toilet? Wanna buy a toilet?'"

A slow smile played out across his face, the same smile I remember from when he figured out how to do fractions before me. His *genius* smile.

"I ever tell you about my uncle Ron? The one who runs a plumbing supply store?"

There were a lot of questions I should have asked at this point, and any one of them could have flushed this whole idea into oblivion. But I was bored, and not too bright.

Getting in was no problem. A plastic tarp was nailed up over the patio doors, where they hadn't installed the glass yet. Not so much breaking and entering as slicing and entering. One quick slash with a box cutter and we were in.

But getting to Black Creek Drive was a different story. Here's where things got seriously stupid. Me and Wayne were thirteen years old. Couldn't drive. So how do we transport the merchandise? You can't strap a toilet to your bike, can't fit it on the bus, can't drag it over a mile down the

sidewalk back to the Jungle. So what's the easiest, most inconspicuous way to get it from point A to point B?

A shopping cart. Now, you never know how loud a shopping cart can be until you push it over uneven pavement, or take it off-road to cut through a vacant lot. My forearms felt numb from the rattling vibration by the time we got to the place. At least the new development had been recently tarred, so our final approach didn't break the sound barrier.

"Don't worry," Wayne told me. "People will just think we're bums collecting pop cans or something."

He had brought an old blanket to cover and cushion the porcelain for our getaway, and a plastic bag of tools for extracting the toilet.

They hadn't hooked up any streetlights yet, so it was real dark, without even a flicker of light from the empty houses.

Choosing one of them at random, we sliced our way in. Setting the flashlight to wide beam, we found two bathrooms upstairs. Since we'd figured the cart had a two-toilet capacity, we couldn't believe our luck. One-stop shopping! I held the light while Wayne went to work.

"Good," he said. "The water isn't hooked up yet. Don't have to worry about a flood."

"Just hurry it up, man." I was getting a queasy feeling in my gut, the same one I remember from when I fell off the roof at my aunt's place one time. The feeling you get in that split second while you're in the air, flying, anticipating the impact.

"Look at this thing," Wayne said. "Extra wide, for the fat butts of the rich."

"Don't these have serial numbers or something?" I asked. "Like cars or guns?"

Wayne grunted as the last of the big nuts came loose.

"That's it," he laughed, getting to his feet. "Easy money. Help me lift it."

You never think how heavy a toilet is until you try and heave it down the hall. We ended up dragging it to the top of the stairs.

"Okay, let's take it slow," Wayne huffed, trying to catch his breath. "I think I'm having a heart attack."

We took the stairs one at a time, facing each other and stepping down sideways. By the fifth step my arms felt like they were going to rip off, and I could feel my own heart attack coming on. My hands were slick with sweat.

I don't know which one of us slipped first, but right then me and Wayne stumbled and gravity worked its magic on the six-hundred-dollar, hundred-pound porcelain baby we were trying to deliver. With the flashlight shining on us from the top of the stairs, we watched the toilet crash down, splintering the hardwood and taking a gouge of plaster out of the wall. The noise boomed through the empty house like a chain reaction of car crashes before the toilet impacted with a final echoing thud on the new wood floor, breaking into three large pieces.

Before the sound died off, blinding light flooded the house. For a second I thought we'd woken someone up, but there was nobody to wake.

"Now, how the hell am I going to write this up?" a strange voice said from downstairs.

Squinting against the sudden brightness, I could make out a cop standing by the light switch, looking from us to the dead toilet, back to us again.

End of story, except for the arrest, the booking, the sentence to an eternity of community service, the humiliation, the restitution and the parental barring of any contact between me and Wayne for the rest of our natural lives (which lasted about eight months—the barring, not our lives).

So that's how my life of crime ended, not with a bang but a flush. Grand theft potty.

"So what's with the new hair?" I ask Wayne, who can't stop rubbing the fresh fuzz on his head.

"Big Boss Man says families don't like bald teens. They think they're skinheads. Bad for business."

"No way," Vinny says, licking chocolate sauce off his spoon. "That's like a violation of your human rights."

"Yeah, well, so is this uniform."

Vinny makes a disgusted grunt. "I mean, what, just because you shave your head you're some neo-Nazi? Is the Dalai Lama a skinhead?"

Wayne frowns. "Who?"

"Is Captain Picard a skinhead?"

"Who?"

I help him out. "The bald guy from *Star Trek*."

"Is Vin Diesel, or what's-his-face from R.E.M., or Charlie Brown, are they skinheads?" Vinny's about to bust a vein in his brain. He's touchy about discrimination.

"Charlie Brown's not really bald. He's got that one hair on his forehead," I say, trying to be helpful.

"Yeah, but that's not real. It's just drawn on," Wayne says.

"Well, he's a cartoon," I tell him. "So *everything* about him is drawn on."

Vinny just shakes his head at Wayne in disgust. "Man, they're walking all over you and you don't even know it."

"Easy for you," I tell him. "You're a bum. Try making a buck."

He shrugs. "I don't buy into this consumer society stuff."

"So that makes you either a bum or a communist," I say.

"Or a free spirit," Vinny says.

"Or a freeloader," I say.

Wayne throws up his hands. "Stop. You guys are making my head hurt. What are you talking about anyway, Duncan? You got that easy job, sitting around all day. No hauling garbage, no mopping up washrooms, no slobs demanding extra sprinkles."

Vinny points at him with his spoon. "Hey, that reminds me, Wayne. Where are my Oreo crumbs?"

"I forgot to scrape them out of the Dumpster. Seriously, this is what I have to deal with all day long."

I'm not really listening to what Wayne's saying. The last few days I've been zoning out right in the middle of things, feeling spacey. It comes from not getting more than a couple hours' sleep every night. At work, Jacob will tell me something and I'll watch his lips move and hear the sound, but the actual words are missing in action. I went through this insomnia thing last year after what happened at the beach, but I thought I'd kicked it. Sometimes I'm so groggy even my teeth feel tired.

"Man, you look like crap," Wayne tells me, shaking me into focus again.

"Thanks for sharing, Wayne."

He scratches at the ketchup stain on his shoulder. "No, I mean it. You look like you haven't slept in a week."

"It's those all-night orgies," I say.

Vinny snorts. "You know, it's not an orgy if you're the only one in the room. There's another word for that."

I shrug. "Some days I just wake up knowing, like deep in my bones, that the world's out to get me. God's got a contract on my head."

They're both staring at me now.

"Get this man a Happy Meal," Vinny says.

"What's the matter with you?" Wayne asks. "The sun used to shine out of your butt."

"Yeah, well, I saw a doctor about that."

"You know what it is?" says Wayne. "It's working five days a week that's doing it—starting to get to me too. What it is—it's like dying one shift at a time."

Vinny sighs. "I feel for you guys."

Wayne tosses his hat at him. "Vinny's an idiot, but he's got the right idea. Be a leech, like him, and no worries. No eight-hour soul-killing shifts. No getting up in the morning. No taking orders."

"No future," I add.

Wayne shakes his head. "Having a future's way over-rated."

He goes on talking, but I'm zoning out again. What I need right now is twelve hours of deep, black, empty sleep.

SIX

Jacob's gone on lunch when the cop comes. He's only a transit cop, but still, he makes me nervous.

"Smells like a tomb down here," he says—his version of hello. "What happened to the old guy?"

I point to the ceiling.

"Dead?" he asks.

"No. Lunch."

He grunts, filling a paper cup at the cooler. "That guy's a sour old fart," he says, swallowing. "Can't really blame him, I guess."

"Why not?"

"Seeing what happened to his wife."

"He's got a wife?"

"Not anymore. She had a stroke, turned into a vegetable. I heard they pulled the plug on her last year." He shrugs. "Sad story."

That stops me cold. My longest conversation with Jacob was on my first day, when he gave me the half-minute tour of the lost and found from his chair at the counter. All I know about him is he's a former subway conductor, running out the clock till retirement.

"Anyway," the cop says, leaning on the other side of the counter. "Someone called in a suspicious package?"

It takes me a second to get what he's saying. I'm still processing Jacob's dead wife.

"Yeah," I say. "It's over here. It was found under a bench at St. Clair Station."

I heave the University of Toronto gym bag up onto the counter. "Suspicious package" covers a lot of ground. Anything *really* suspicious, like a gun or a suitcase of cocaine, never makes it down to us. We only get the stuff that's borderline.

Like this. A gym bag full of gas masks.

The cop grunts. "Kinky."

"Jacob was the one who called up. He was saying how they had those terrorist gas attacks on the subway over in Japan, some cult thing."

He digs around in the bag to see what else is in there. One piece of advice Jacob gave me my first day: never stick your hand where you can't see where it's going. Needles and knives, and one time a rat, are some of the nasty things Jacob's discovered hiding in bags and pockets.

"The old man's got an active imagination," the cop tells me. "These are probably for some student protest or something."

I shrug. "You going to take it?"

He weighs the bag in his right hand. "Guess so. I'm gonna have to haul it all the way uptown."

As he leaves, he says, "Call me when you find something interesting—a pipe bomb, or a severed head. That I can work with."

Then he's gone and I can relax. I guess I'm just paranoid, but I always think they *know*. Cops, I mean. That they can tell, the way a dog can smell fear, that I'm this major felon. The thing with the stolen toilet is a *juvie* crime, which means it's wiped from my record when I hit eighteen, but still—they've got my fingerprints on file somewhere. After they printed us, the cops gave us paper towels to clean off the ink, but all that did was smudge the ink around. When my parents came to pick me up I kept my hands fisted so they wouldn't see the black stains. It took a good half hour scrubbing away a few layers of skin to lose the ink.

About what the cop said, it kind of makes sense now— why Jacob, who must have three decades on the job, has been exiled to this underground armpit to run out his time. He must have asked for it.

I pick a half-sized kids' basketball off the top of an over-flowing box of sports equipment and dribble down the aisle. After you tune out the rumble of the passing trains you realize how quiet it is down here. Even the sound of the drib-bling gets swallowed up by the debris stacked on the shelves.

What's it like seeing someone you love die like that, in slow motion? What's it like being left with just a body, its heart still beating for no reason?

Things I can't ask Jacob. The kind of questions that come to you working down here in the dungeon.

I try to sink a shot, using an upturned lampshade for a basket. But I just don't have the touch. Bouncing off the rim, the ball rolls away and I have to chase it down the aisle. Digging it out from where it's wedged under a bottom shelf, my eyes fall on the boxes of lost books. The ball pulls free and I blow the dust off it. Next to my foot on the floor, the brown leather book with no title lies where I kicked it the other day.

I pass the ball from hand to hand, wanting to turn and dribble back to the counter. But somehow the command never makes it from my brain to my legs.

I'll just look and see if there's a name inside the cover, an address or something. Why, I don't know. What am I going to do about it? Sticking the ball under my arm, I reach down and grab the book. From the date on the Post-it stuck to the cover I see it came in ten days ago.

The feel of the soft, worn leather makes me cringe—feels too much like skin.

I turn to the beginning, with the mice and the drowning times. There's no name on it anywhere. Flipping through the pages, past the newspaper clippings about the dead cats, I come across handwritten passages. A lot of it makes no sense to me; it's like he's ranting in his own little code. But then he'll string a few understandable paragraphs together.

Crack slaves and whores been using this boarded-up hotel to crash. Didn't need the crowbar to get in. Climbed the fire escape and squeezed through a broken window. *Junkies and skanks are good cover. Cops will blame them and their pipes for the fire. Using thinner this time. They'll think it's left over from the sniffers and huffers. The hotel's a skeleton, stripped. Ripe for burning.*

THREE LADDER TRUCKS RESPONDING. THREE COP CARS. TWO AMBULANCES. BIG CROWD. FEEL THE HEAT A BLOCK AWAY.

There's a folded article stapled to the next page. I open it up.

SUSPICIOUS FIRE DESTROYS REGENT HOTEL, it says. Below the headline is a picture of a four-story building swallowed by flames.

The basketball falls from under my arm and rolls away. I feel a tremendous urge to rip this leather-bound book of mental diarrhea into confetti—to destroy it and the warped mind it came from. Behind the words there's this big nothing where a conscience should be, a black hole sucking you down into the dark.

And no name. Nothing to put a face on the cockroach who wrote it.

Up front, I hear the door closing. I step over to the next aisle so I can have a clear view to the counter.

"I'm back," Jacob calls out.

My turn to go on lunch.

"So, they come for the gas masks?" he asks when I walk up.

I nod. "He said he's sure it's nothing, but he took it anyway."

"Hah!" Jacob grunts his disgust, settling into the grooves he's worked into his seat. "Bunch of know-nothing pretend cops. One drop of sarin gas can kill a thousand people."

I only shrug, not wanting to argue chemistry and death right now. "He said to call when we find a pipe bomb, or someone's head."

"Now they're comedians. Wait till something really bad happens—and it will—while they're off busting turnstile jumpers."

"Yeah," I grunt.

"What's that you got there?" he asks.

I look down to see that I'm still holding the diary. Every part of me wants to flush or burn the thing, but I can't. Right now, I couldn't tell you why. I should trash it, but that wouldn't really do anything. It would still be in my head, and the psycho who wrote it would still be out there walking the streets.

"It's nothing," I tell him. "Just a blank book."

"Whatever. You're on lunch now."

I nod, half hearing his words, wondering what I'm supposed to do with this thing.

SEVEN

"I'm dying, man," Wayne tells me on the phone. He's always dying. He gets hungry—he's dying. Gets thirsty—dying. Bored—dying. "I'm burning up in here. Stick a fork in me. I'm done."

"So what are you thinkin'?"

"Let's hit the pool," Wayne says.

"The pool?"

"Yeah. You know, the hole in the ground filled with water and fifty gallons of chlorine?"

"It's after five o'clock," I say. "Isn't it a little late for the pool?"

"Not too late for me to spontaneously combust. The pool's open till sunset."

I used to live at the pool every summer. This year I haven't gone once. Maybe it's the nightmares spooking me. But right now it's too hot to be scared.

"Okay," I say. "I'll be over in ten minutes. I'm gonna call Vinny. See if he's coming."

"He never comes. In the whole history of Vinny, has he ever gone swimming with us?"

I give him a shrug he can't see over the phone.

"Whatever," Wayne says. "Just hurry up. Because I'm—"

"Dying. I know. I'm hurrying."

When Vinny picks up, he tells me what I already know. "I can't swim."

"Can't swim?" I say. Anybody can swim. Before we were apes, we were fish. I don't tell Vinny about the fish thing because his nickname in school—what the idiots call him—is Flipper. Because of his left arm.

"Okay, it's not that I can't swim. I used to when I was a kid. It's just, I'm not gonna have everybody staring at me and freaking out."

"Yeah, I guess you have a point."

"Big joke, right?" Vinny says. "Flipper won't swim."

I grunt at that. When it comes to his arm, Vinny's always ready to pick a fight.

"Besides, there's more urine in those pools than chlorine," he tells me.

"Thanks, you're really putting me in the mood now. See you later."

I knew calling him to go with us was a waste of time, but I guess I'm kind of stalling. The thought of going in the water again—even just the pool—is giving me this nauseous feeling. I almost pick up the phone to call Wayne back and cancel. But then I shake it off.

Just get over it, I tell myself.

Mom's on the couch in the living room with the big fan blasting her. Her homework takes up most of the coffee table, the scattered papers held down against the breeze with a half-dozen paperweights. The weights are flat skipping stones gathered from the lakeshore and defaced with paintings of cats chasing butterflies and kittens sniffing soap bubbles, that kind of stuff. Mom buys them at a little store on Center Island. "I can't resist," she explains. "They're so wonderfully tacky."

"What's all this?" I ask, slumping beside her on the couch to steal some of the breeze.

"I have an essay due Friday." She highlights a paragraph in *The New Geography: World in Transition*.

I shake my head. "Why bother?"

"What do you mean?"

"I don't know. You gonna be a geographer when you grow up?"

It's an old argument. Mom works part-time up at the Wal-Mart, making a few bucks over minimum. I don't get why she takes these courses over at the community college. I mean, she's got brains, but she's not exactly on the fast track for making the faculty at Oxford or anything.

"Haven't you ever wanted to know something new? For no reason, just to know it? Expand your mind?"

"Hmmm . . ." I consider it. "Well . . . no! I've spent the last decade having my brain stretched against my will. It's been stretched so much, it's like an old pair of underwear with the elastic all shot."

"That's a lovely image," she says, trying to finish the page she's on.

Wayne vows he'll never read another book for the rest of his life after he graduates. But then I don't know if he's ever actually finished one yet, so that's not saying much. He invented this system where you only read every fourth page of a book, so it's only a quarter as long. But he still doesn't know what the verdict was at the end of *To Kill a Mockingbird,* or what happened to Gatsby, or if the old man in *The Old Man and the Sea* ever made it back to shore.

"This is madness," I tell her.

"It's the opposite of madness. You learn something new, you'll be somebody new."

"Can I be Brad Pitt?"

Without taking her eyes off the page, Mom reaches over with her marker and highlights my elbow.

"Quit bugging me," she says.

"Okay. I'm outta here."

I get up and grab my shoes. As I'm putting them on by the door, I call out, "Hey, Mom. What's it called when you're afraid of water?"

"That's . . . hydrophobia. Why do you ask?"

I heave out a sigh, trying to lose the queasy feeling in my gut. "No reason."

MAXIMUM CAPACITY: 200

That's what the sign says, but I guess nobody told the guy selling tickets. It's after six o'clock, and you'd think people would be home eating dinner or something. But the pool looks like rush hour on the subway—armpit to armpit, can't do a backstroke without whacking someone in the head.

Before you get to the pool you have to go through these outdoor showers, which for some reason they set to subzero temperatures.

I run through. But Wayne, just to show who's the man, stands under there and takes it.

"Probably the first shower you've had in weeks," I say.

He makes a face. "I could stay here all day," he says, but you can tell he's holding back the shivers.

"You're turning blue," I tell him.

"It's good for the heart." Wayne's voice breaks as he steps out.

The pool stretches from the baby end, where you're lucky if you even get your toes damp, to the deep end, where giant squids have been spotted.

Little kids are squealing and screaming.

The sun burns the shower-freeze out of us real quick.

"Okay," Wayne says, stopping ten feet from the edge. "On three."

It's this thing we've been doing for forever. We jump in synch, two cannonballs hitting the water at the same time, splashing a tidal wave out onto the sunbathers lying out of reach (they think) on their towels back near the fence. Me, I think we're getting too old for it. But Wayne's going to be out here when he's eighty, cannonballing in a wheelchair.

A momentary space opens up in the crowded pool.

"Onetwothree," Wayne shouts, sprinting for the edge.

The trick is to hit the water at just the right angle, throwing the wave out in the perfect direction without breaking another swimmer's spine in the process. It's a science. One quick breath when I'm launching into the air, bringing my knees up to hug them to my chest. Then I shut my eyes and brace for impact.

The thing about cannonballing is you never get to see your own splash. It's like throwing a punch and never seeing it land. When I come back up and blink my eyes clear, I can tell our aim was good. Two bikini'd girls are sitting up, staring death at us.

"Sorry!" Wayne calls to them, but his laughter erases the apology.

"Better watch out," I tell him. "Bigfoot's on duty."

Bigfoot is the main lifeguard. She's here every year, way up on the tall chair, looking down on us from behind mirrored sunglasses. It's impossible to tell who she's looking at with those things on, and I think that's the point. She's all-seeing. She's not Bigfoot because of her feet; it's her legs. We're talking hairy. We're talking scary hairy.

Wayne pulls our locker key from the inside pocket of his trunks. He holds it up between us and drops it into the water.

"Ooops," he says. "Dropped it."

I roll my eyes. You know, we grew up together— Hold it, that's not saying it right. I grew up. Wayne just got older. He's the oldest seven-year-old on the planet. He's looking at me now like a puppy, waiting for me to dive first so he can try and beat me to it.

"Man, that is so old," I tell him.

"Maybe. But we're going to be walking home in our trunks if we don't get it back."

It's a standoff. Like JFK and that Russian guy in the Cuban Missile Crisis. The question is, who's going to blink first. Who's going to be the winner, the JFK. And who'll be the Russian guy.

"That's a long walk," I say. "With no shoes."

"And no Slurpee money," Wayne adds.

"Oh well." I stroke over to the side and lean an arm, real casual, on the edge. "What're you gonna do?"

Wayne swims to the edge on the other side. He shrugs at me. I shrug back.

"Slurpee would have been nice," I shout over.

"It's a real shame," he calls, shaking his head.

Bigfoot blows her earsplitting whistle at some kid trying to climb the fence to get in free. Those mirrored shades miss nothing.

Wayne's distracted, twisted around to see what's going on. So I decide to give in and play the game one more time. I dive, kicking off the side of the pool.

It's a different world down here. No more squealing and splashing. Sunlight breaks up into waving bands on the bottom.

At its deepest, the pool reaches ten feet. It only takes a

few strokes to get down there; then I start searching for the silver key. I've been practicing holding my breath, stretching my lungs, since I was a kid. But it's been a while since I've been in the water. I quit the swim team last year, told them I was too busy. I figure I've got at least a minute before I have to head back up. Something glints by the stripe marking a depth of nine feet, but it's just a penny, left over from someone else's game.

Crawling along the bottom like a crab, I almost miss it. The key doesn't shine like the penny did. I pick it up and start to turn for the surface when something grabs my foot.

I know it's Wayne, trying to make me drop the key. It's just him. I know that. But my heart starts jackhammering.

The sun seems to go behind a cloud, throwing me into shadow. A second later it blacks out completely, like some kind of sudden freak eclipse.

My ears pick up a sound carried through the water, too distant to make out, but building with every spasm of my heart. It grows louder and higher as it gets closer. I turn in the water, trying to break away from the hand on my foot. The sound is coming from every direction.

A scream. A long, torn-out scream.

Above me, the legs of the swimmers hang down. They're moving limply, all together, in synch. Like there's no life in them, and they're only moving with the waves like seaweed.

I can't look down. Because the hand on my foot isn't Wayne's anymore. It's too cold to be a living hand.

The scream is everywhere, surrounding me and pressing

in as if it has a physical presence, trying to squeeze the breath out of me. I fight my way up in a blind panic, kicking and flailing my arms. A sound tears out of me like an answer to the scream blasting through the water. A strangled sound that uses up the last of my air.

As I break the surface, all that's left of my own scream is a choked gasp.

The sun's back, burning an intense white from a clear blue sky. My head whips around, expecting bodies floating facedown. But everybody's laughing, splashing, and alive.

Wayne pops up beside me.

"Are you nuts?" he says. "You kicked me in the chest."

I swim over to the side and pull myself out.

"Where you going?" Wayne asks.

"I'm done," I tell him, my teeth chattering in the baking heat.

"We just got here."

I hurry away from the edge toward the exit, not even looking to see if Wayne's following. My right hand is clenched in a tight fist, and when I open it I see the stupid locker key. I've been squeezing it so hard there's a tiny cut where the metal broke the skin. A drop of blood trickles down my wrist.

I hold my breath rushing back through the showers to the locker rooms, barely feeling the icy bite of the water. After what I saw in the pool, I'm already cold to the bone.

EIGHT

Back in the stacks, I'm supposed to be going through expiration dates and packing stuff for the sale. Standing by my lawn chair, I consider my options. A little handball against the back wall, some light reading, or snooping through the lost suitcases and briefcases. Jacob doesn't care. He reads his papers, does a jumble or a crossword, and listens to the afternoon baseball games on his pocket radio.

My eyes come to rest on that putrid diary again. What to do with it? I grab a seat and reluctantly pick it up, opening it to where I left off.

After the hotel fire there's another clipping that says: ARSON SUSPECTED IN USED BOOKSTORE FIRE. The accompanying photo shows a low-rise engulfed in thick black smoke. A scribbled note in the margin reads: *No accelerant needed with all that paper. Maybe thirty cops and firemen responding.*

The bell rings twice. I flinch like someone just cattle-prodded me. The legs of the lawn chair scrape against the cement floor as I get up and set the open book facedown on top of a box.

Whoever said burning books was wrong never read this one.

"Looking for a golf club," Jacob tells me at the desk.

"It's a putter," says a bright-eyed guy in a suit. He stands there, his hair gelled to perfection, drumming his fingers on his briefcase lying on the counter.

"It's got a red leather grip," he tells me. "And on the top it says 'ninety-nine finalist.'"

"Okay, I'll take a look," I say.

Great, now I'm going to lose my putter. I've been practicing with it, using a box of Ping-Pong balls someone left behind on the subway. My putting green is the cement floor. For a hole I've been using a *Star Trek* collector's glass (Mr. Sulu, in case you're wondering). Been getting pretty good at it too, even with the floor being a little slanted and all.

Back in the sports equipment aisle, I hold the club fondly, feeling the red leather grip. '99 FINALIST is engraved right there on the base. I take a couple practice swings, sinking imaginary Ping-Pong balls. I was hoping this beauty would stay safe here until its time expired, so I could give it a nice home.

"This the one?" I ask, back at the counter.

His bright eyes brighten another hundred watts. "That's her."

The whole time I've been handling that putter I never knew it was a *she*.

"I won this in the national tournament," he tells us,

holding the club up horizontally so he can sight down its length and make sure it hasn't been warped.

"You play pro golf?" I ask.

"Pro *miniature* golf," he says. "I won the city championship that year, and went all the way to the national finals."

Jacob gives me a sidelong glance, rolls his eyes.

"Didn't know they had pro Putt-Putt," I say. "Is there any money in it?"

"Some. When you get to the *nationals*."

He frowns, holding the bottom of the club up to the light. Probably scratched from my putting with it on cement. For some reason this makes me happy. This guy goes through life with his perfect hair and shining eyes. Like life's a dream. He could use a little scratch on his perfection.

Man, Wayne was right. I *do* need a Happy Meal.

Jacob makes Mr. Putt-Putt sign for the club in the register. When he's gone, Jacob looks over from his paper. "I don't think I've ever been that clean."

I smile, shaking my head. Me neither.

Jacob so rarely talks to me when it's not absolutely necessary that I'm always too much in shock to follow up on it.

So I wander back to my lawn chair and pick the book up where I left off.

The actual handwriting in the diary seems to change the deeper I get into it, becoming neater, more mature. My guess is he's been writing in it for years, the misspellings and mistakes growing more scarce. It's a thick book; two hundred pages maybe.

As I read on, the fires get bigger and better. He goes into detail about how many fire trucks show up, the number of cop cars, how the fire advances. He must have been standing on the sidelines watching every one of his creations. His descriptions of the flames are almost pornographic. Real wet-dream stuff for the criminally insane.

It's not the kind of diary where he'll describe his day. It reads more like a rap sheet, a journal of his crimes. There'll be page after page of clippings that span an eight-month period, but nothing about what happened in his life during that time.

Enough of this! I skip ahead to the later parts of the diary to see how this twisted tale turns out.

This is kids' stuff, he writes after detailing another arson. *Need something BIGGER.*

Then a few pages farther on:

Been hunting. Riding the subway, searching the faces for the right one. All the pretty ladies sitting across from me. It's like an audition. A cattle call.

The air stirs around me, just the slightest draft from a train passing through one of the tunnels overhead, but it sends a chill through me that raises the short hairs on my forearms.

Hunting. He's hunting. He's moved past the animals and the fires. The "kids' stuff." Now he's going after bigger game. The real thing. A woman.

NINE

Dragging myself out of bed a little before noon on Saturday, I feel all twisted and sweaty, like I've just spent a few hours tossing around in a straightjacket. Passing by my parents' room, I can hear the two big fans inside on high, blasting with the power of twin jet engines.

Dad will still be sleeping. He started working the grave-yard shift last week. That's midnight to eight in the morning. Then he comes home, showers, has a bite, and collapses into bed. Dad calls it the vampire shift—up at night, back in the coffin by nine A.M. It's the weekend, but he tries to stick to his backward schedule or he'll be all screwed up on Monday.

He's a machinist at a factory that makes catalogues for Lands' End and Abercrombie & Fitch. For eight hours a day, he walks the length of an assembly machine half a block long. It jams; he unjams it. It breaks; he fixes it.

I don't have to be real quiet. Dad uses heavy-duty earplugs to block out the sounds of the Jungle. He also wears a blackout mask over his eyes to fool his body into believing it's night. You could shoot off a cannon and fire off a flare and he wouldn't stop snoring.

In the kitchen, Mom's got the thick Saturday edition of the *Toronto Star* laid out on the table.

"Hey, Sleeping Beauty," she says.

"Hmm," I grunt. "What's for breakfast?"

"Breakfast was three hours ago. You snooze, you lose. I had French toast."

She's wearing her I RAN THE 2001 TORONTO MARATHON T-shirt. She does that kind of stuff—exercises. Those healthy genes must have skipped my generation.

"What about your poor starving son?" I ask.

"What do you want me to do, regurgitate something? There's sandwiches in the fridge."

Mom makes two kinds of meals. There's food we can eat, and then there's stuff only Dad can stomach. When he gets home, he stinks of binding glue and oil. The glue kills his sense of smell and numbs his taste buds. Everything he eats has to be spicy or it tastes like mud.

So one sandwich has a red *H* written on the foil. *H* for *hot*. Dad's latest obsession is Spontaneous Combustion hot sauce—makes his eyes water when he eats.

I grab a normal nonflammable one and a Coke. What I need is a caffeine IV drip pumping straight into my arm. Removing the sandwich from its foil, I peel back the bread and examine the contents.

"It's meat loaf," she tells me.

I take a small bite. "Try again?" I say.

Mom sighs. "Okay, it's tofu loaf. We've got a cholesterol problem in this place. One good pastrami sandwich will move your father into heart-attack country. You don't like it—"

"Hey, hey, I just like to know what I'm eating."

"Well then, eat up and shut up. Sweetie," she adds, to soften the blow.

I read the comics as I eat. You can't trust tofu. I mean, you never see it out in the wild, like a cow or a banana or a zucchini. *Tofu*—even the word sounds weird, like someone sneezing in another language.

She turns a page. "You were making noises in your sleep again last night," she says quietly.

I stop chewing. "What kind of noises?"

"Oh, you know, kind of . . . whimpering."

I swallow. "Wasn't loud, was it?"

She shakes her head. "I only noticed because I don't sleep all that well alone, with your father on graveyard."

She hands me a paper towel a second before I realize I need one. "You've got mustard all over your face," Mom tells me. She sets her paper down and grabs some o.j. from the fridge. "I was watching this nature special last night—penguins down at the South Pole. After the mating season there are thousands and thousands of little baby penguins that all look exactly alike. And they're all crying out for food. Not unlike yourself." She reaches across the table and gives me a little shove. "So the mothers go diving for fish. And when they come back up, there are all these babies crying out for lunch. And how is the mother supposed to find her screaming baby in a mob of identical screaming babies? But *every* time she knows exactly which crying penguin is her crying penguin. It's a mother's hearing, tuned to that one specific frequency."

"Which means?" I ask.

"Means I only have ears for you, baby." She smiles as I groan. "So you want to talk about it?"

I shrug. "Nothing to talk about. Dreams," I say, shaking my head, like they have no power over me.

Mom worries too much—those ears permanently tuned in to me. Late last year she made me go see a psychiatrist a couple of times, back when I wasn't sleeping at all. He gave me some pills. They put me out—no dreams, no thoughts, no brain, no pain. But they left me groggy and a little dizzy, so I stopped taking them. Sometimes pain is better than nothing.

"I'm here," she tells me when I don't say any more. "Always here."

"I know." I give her a sleepy smile.

She turns to the travel section of the newspaper.

"You ever think of giving Kim a call?" she asks.

"No. That's been over for forever."

"I know. But she was good for you."

"Yeah. Guess I just wasn't good for her."

I take a long drink.

"You know, that Coke is going to burn a hole in your stomach," Mom tells me.

"I just hope it kills the tofu first."

I read somewhere—or maybe I saw it in a movie—how people who lose a leg or an arm can still feel the missing limb sometimes. They'll get this impossible itch on a foot that isn't there anymore, or they'll feel an ache where there's nothing left to ache. They call it a phantom limb, because of the ghost pains it still sends back to the brain.

That's what Kim is like for me now—my phantom girl-friend. Gone, but still aching.

And whenever I feel like waking up the ghost, I pull out the old photos.

The thing is, these shots flatten her into two dimensions and freeze her in time. And that's definitely not Kim. She's always in motion. I've got pictures of her last summer over on Center Island, where they've got an amusement park and a working farm you can walk through. The way I remember it she was just exploding, really *alive*. Trying to swallow everything in a day, like she only had hours to live.

But I'm looking at those photos now and all I see is someone who fits her general description. Whatever makes Kim *Kim* got lost in translation. The only shot that says any-thing about what she's like is one where she moved when I was clicking. She's a blond blur, rushing out of the frame.

Kim plays center for Milton High's girls' basketball team.

They call her Big Bird, because she's almost six feet tall and has wild, feathery blond hair. I liked the tallness of her, the longness of her; I felt like an explorer, going over her body. There was this vanilla-scented oil she always wore, made me think of ice cream, made me think of licking her behind her ears.

We were together about a year. Where it went wrong, where I screwed it all up, was after Kayuga Beach.

Kim started volunteering at Gatherup, a drop-in center for street kids downtown. It's run by a guy named Father Darcy out of the Osgood community center. He's a priest, but he's okay. He doesn't throw Bibles at you or anything.

I told her spending time there was a bad idea.

"Can't you volunteer somewhere else?" I said to her. "That place is a real hole."

We were shooting free throws in back of the Jungle, where somebody had screwed a hoop into the bricks about ten feet up. You couldn't really dribble with all the cracks and bumps in the asphalt, so we played twenty-one. She spotted me ten. I was still losing.

"They don't need me somewhere else," Kim said. "They need me there."

I took my shot and bounced it off the bricks.

"You're not following through," she told me. She showed me how, making the motion without the ball, bending her wrists.

I passed her the ball. "Yeah, yeah. Just take your shot, Birdy."

She did, sinking the ball without it even touching the rim.

"I mean, that drop-in place," I said. "It's like right beside a needle exchange."

"The exchange is three blocks over."

I took my time, lining up my shot. "So what do you do down there?"

"Give out information. You know, about places to stay, free meals, drug treatment."

"Don't they have social workers for that?"

"Yeah, but a lot of kids are scared to talk to them. Scared they'll get turned in and sent home against their will. Or worse, to foster care. I've heard some real horror stories."

My shot bounced off the rim.

"Maybe I should spot you twenty next time," Kim said, chasing down the rebound. She caught up with it and started dribbling the ball on the broken asphalt, between and around her legs, making it look easy.

"I don't like you being down there," I said. "I mean, these are street kids. You can't trust them. They'd probably knife you for the change in your pockets."

She stopped dribbling, giving me a look I was getting a lot from her. The *stranger* look, like she wasn't sure who I was anymore. She kept saying I was turning into this mass of negative energy.

"Most of the kids there are lost and scared," she said. "What I do is listen to them, pass out cookies and coffee. And besides, they have security in the center. I'm not an idiot. I can read a situation and know when to back off."

"Tell me when you're getting off and I'll pick you up."

Kim was frowning. "I already told you, I don't need you to pick me up. The security guys will walk with me to the subway if I need them. It's only half a block."

I looked up at the brick wall, waiting for her to take another shot. The last few weeks, her team had been running practices after school, so I'd been meeting up with her to walk her home. It was late October and getting dark earlier.

"Just tell me when—"

"No," she said. "This has to stop. You're my boyfriend, not my bodyguard."

I shake my head, telling her, "You just don't know . . . what's out there."

She sighed. "The world's out there, Duncan. The good, the bad, and the plain old ugly. I can't go around being afraid all the time."

"I don't want you to."

"Yes, you do." Her voice broke, and she had to take a deep breath to steady herself. "You've locked yourself up in some dark little prison cell. And you want me to join you. But I can't live like that."

Her eyes were tearing up. That seemed to happen a lot back then when we talked.

I whispered, "No." No to her crying, to what she was saying, to everything. She wrapped her long arms around me, dropping the ball to hug me.

I didn't know it then, but that was the beginning of the

end. It took a while; things got messy. I don't know if there was an exact time of death for our relationship; one day I woke up and it just wasn't there anymore.

I still see her sometimes, passing in the halls at Milton. We say hi and everything, but it's nothing like before.

It's a phantom.

TEN

Traffic noise and the distant but relentless beat of dance music drift in through my open window. But not even a hint of a breeze. It's past midnight. I'm sitting at my desk in my underwear, with a fan aimed at my head. In front of me is the diary.

At the top of the page it says: 3 CONTESTANTS. Under that heading are three names: Cherry, Bones, and Clown. Details are listed for each woman: their clothing, hair and makeup, approximate height and weight.

Cherry is a redhead. Bones is anorexically thin. Clown wears heavy makeup.

He's got this down to a science—another one of his experiments. He dissects them with his eyes.

For each woman, he has times listed for when they show up, at which subway stations. What stop they get on at and where they get off. He's got their schedules mapped out. This guy must spend hours on the trains, hunting.

From their descriptions, they're all white and in their late teens to early twenties. Thin and small and pale. That seems to be his thing. He talks about seeing something in their eyes, a vulnerability, a weakness. *Stray dogs,* he calls them at one point. *Alley dogs, licking the hands of strangers.*

He scrawls a note to himself: *Pick strangers.*

Somewhere in these pages is the answer, a way to track him down. There's nothing that gives his identity away, no convenient nameplate at the front: *This book belongs to . . .*

I need a name, he writes at one point. I've got one for him: Roach. Plain and simple, as ugly and descriptive as the tags he gives his targets. An insect that hides from the light.

I lean back in my chair and stare at the ceiling, where a fly is beating its brains out against the bare lightbulb.

I've got to think. What do I do with this? Give it to the cops? And what will they do? There's no name here, nothing to put a face on this nut. Will they even believe it? Maybe they'll say it's fiction, someone's overactive imagination. Can't arrest somebody for a thought. What do I really have here? A collection of psychotic dreams set down on paper. The potential stalking of unknown women. They would just file it in a drawer somewhere. Like the transit cop said, a pipe bomb or a severed head they can deal with. But going through some wacko's diary trying to decipher fantasy from reality—forget about it.

And my fingerprints are all over this book. What if they think it's me? I've got a record for a breaking and entering. I'm already dirty in their eyes.

No. I can't go to them.

I squeeze my eyes shut, trying to think. I can hear the soft plinking sound of the fly's assault on the bulb.

Then it comes to me. The answer. And it feels like all the broken parts inside me are coming together, fitting into place.

Maybe *I'm* supposed to find him! It makes sense, so clear and perfect. I'm the one who found the diary. For a reason. This is my second chance.

Real faint, sounding in the back of my brain like the echo of an echo, one of those broken parts of me says: *That's crazy. It's too late to save the drowned girl.*

But maybe that's why she keeps coming back in my dreams, to remind me. It's like when you get turned around deep underwater and you can't even tell which way is up anymore. That's why she's come back—to show me the way up to the surface again.

Maybe I'm the only one who can save these women.

I get up and shift the fan around so it's aimed at my bed. Turning off the light, I end the epic battle of the fly versus the lightbulb. I'm hoping to find some cool escape in the dark. Kicking the sheets off the bed, I lie there in my underwear, blinking at the ceiling and the play of headlights on it from cars passing in the street below. A plan squeaks into place in my rusty brain.

Find his targets, and I might just find Roach, too. I have their times, subway stops, and what they look like. So I track them down, watch, and wait for him to show.

It's not a good plan, but it's the only one I've got. In a way that's too horrible to think about right now, they're the bait.

I just have to find them before he bites.

ELEVEN

"What a piece of crap," Vinny says.

He's talking about the movie we just saw, Schwarzenegger's new comedy. We're walking down Yonge Street to the subway. Downtown is loud and smoggy tonight, the heat holding the exhaust fumes close to the ground.

Vinny's talking way too loud. He's on a caffeine high, thanks to an extra-large Coke and a big bag of M&M's.

"Keep it down," I tell him. "You're scaring the civilians."

I met up with Vin after work. He's been waiting for this movie since last year. At home he's got the entire Schwarzenegger collection from *Hercules in New York* to *Terminator 3*. Over the years he's made me watch them all— even the documentaries from Arnold's old bodybuilding days. Vin's got this obsession with muscles, probably because he doesn't have any.

"That was two hours long and he didn't kill anybody," Vin says. "What a waste of all that muscle. He's a seven-time Mr. Olympia, what the hell's he doing cracking jokes?"

"Well, the guy's getting old. What is he, sixty?"

"Fifty-six."

"So he's gotta take it easy sometime," I tell him. "Who wants to see the Terminator as a senior citizen, getting a walker and fishing his dentures out of his soup?"

Vinny ignores me and starts tearing into the plot of Arnie's latest. Schwarzenegger's always been his god, and when your god screws up he's got a lot farther to fall than the rest of us.

Vin's *so* wired. It's going to take a real effort not to push him into traffic.

I let my brain escape to another frequency, grunting now and then to show I'm hanging in there with him. I've got bigger things to worry about than Arnie's comedic timing. I have a plan for tonight.

The sun set a little while ago, and the clouds are purple-red, their color intensified by the smog. The cool of the theater is a distant memory, smothered by the breathless summer night. Vinny's going on now about the genius of *The Terminator*, the first one, with Schwarzenegger hunting down Linda Hamilton to prevent her unborn son from saving the future.

Hunting. The word sticks in my mind.

My plan for tonight is to track down Roach. I don't have it all worked out, but I figure I'll just follow the blueprints he's laid out in his diary.

". . . he's this perfect killing machine," Vinny says.

That startles me for a second. It's like Vin's been reading

my mind. But then I realize he's still talking about the Terminator.

In my back pocket is a photocopy of Roach's target list. I'm going to follow his little treasure map, see where it leads. But the thing is, who knows if he's picked out new targets by now? Or—

Or if he's already done it!

I stop dead on the sidewalk. The noise of traffic suddenly seems far away. What if I'm already too late? The thought knocks the wind out of me. A police siren in the distance filters through my brain, sounding like a scream rising and falling somewhere out of reach.

The early-evening crowds push past as I make my way over to the curb to lean on a parking meter. I try to shake the fog out of my head, but getting a lungful of exhaust doesn't help. I have to squeeze my eyes shut and make a supreme effort to hold on to the meter.

"What's going on?" Vinny's voice is buried under the roar of a passing truck.

Don't lose it now, I tell myself. Don't give up.

No! He can't have made his move already. I'd know if he had. Somehow I'd know. Deep in a corner of my brain I realize how crazy and desperate that sounds. But I hold on to the thought—it's the only thing steadying me.

I'm not too late. I can't be! The diary got turned in about two weeks ago, and he was still planning then, building up to it.

Get a grip.

"Duncan. Man, what's going on?"

When I open my eyes again, Vinny's frowning at me like I've gone nuts. Who knows, maybe I'm halfway there.

"Sorry," I say. "I must have ate something bad. That fried chicken we had."

"Yeah? I don't feel anything."

I inhale some more toxic fumes as the noise of the city rushes back in on me. "You didn't have the coleslaw."

Vinny keeps an eye on me as we cross Yonge and head down the stairs to the subway. The breeze from an arriving train blows past us, a breath of stale air.

"You gonna chuck?" Vinny asks.

"You'll be the first to know," I promise him.

We get hung up in line at the ticket booth and have to wait for the next train. Vin stands on the edge of the platform, staring down the tunnel for any sign of light. But in the subway, before you see anything, you feel it. A vibration in the concrete, the air stirring. Like something's waking up in the dark down there.

Vin yawns wide enough to fit a billiard ball in his mouth.

"Miss your nap today?" I ask.

He stretches and groans. "They're doing all that construction down the block, starting up at seven in the freaking morning."

I examine one of the benches on the platform to make sure it's safe to sit. It's been graffiti tagged so many times it looks like an abstract painting. I collapse onto it, stretching out my legs. I'm working on zero sleep here. Vinny doesn't know the meaning of tired. My eyes feel itchy, making me squint a little.

"Condos," I say.

"Huh?"

"That's the construction up our block. They're building condos on Keele Street."

Vinny barks a laugh. "Who's going to buy a condo next to the Jungle? I mean, what a view!"

"I'm sure they'll put a barbed-wire fence around the new place to keep us out."

"Barbed wire won't stop the noise."

My head's clearing up now. I push all my doubts way back in my brain where I won't have to hear them whispering. I think too much. I have to start *doing* more, thinking less.

"We gotta get out of that place," he says.

Before he came to the Jungle, Vin lived in a nice house out in Scarborough. But his parents divorced, it got ugly, and he and his mom ended up with next to nothing.

"What've you got against the Jungle?" I ask.

"It's a dead end. A sinkhole."

"Yeah. So what's your point?"

"It's the duty of every prisoner of war to try and escape," he says.

"What war? What prison?"

Vinny kicks a crumpled Mountain Dew can down the platform. "The war against the lower class. It's the largest undeclared war in modern history."

"Oh, man," I groan. "Don't start up with that stuff again. I'm sorry I asked."

Vinny's a rebel with too many causes. He's going to be a professional protester when he grows up.

"They keep us out of sight in slums and ghettos. Keep us down with minimum wage and crappy schools. They numb our brains with fast food and five hundred channels. All because they need drones to do their dirty work."

I nod. I've heard this speech before. "Because *somebody's* got to work at McDonald's," I say, deciding to agree with him to stop his rant.

"Exactly!"

"Next time you're getting the caffeine-free Coke," I tell him. "And never again am I letting you near the big bag of M&M's."

He just shakes his head, wandering over to the edge of the platform.

Sure, I want to escape the Jungle. For Mom and Dad, what started out as a pit stop there turned permanent. That scares the crap out of me. Mom started my college fund when I was still doing somersaults in her stomach. Dad keeps telling me I've got her brains and his devastating good looks. I've got a *future*, so they tell me.

"Man, look at those things," Vinny says.

"What things?"

He nods toward the tracks. "Rats. There's like a whole civilization down here."

I get up and join him on the edge.

Rats. Small and quick, speeding gray shadows. There's poison set under the platform overhang and in the tunnels, even in the lost and found. But they breed faster than they die. When the subway shuts down around one A.M., the tunnels are theirs. They own the night.

"There's supposed to be more of *them* in the city than us," Vinny says.

I watch a mangy one crawl over the tracks to sink its teeth into a hot dog bun. When the air stirs just the smallest bit, it stops eating and raises its nose, smelling for danger. Then the sound approaches, like thunder rolling toward us. The rat knows the drill. As the train's headlights pull into view around a curve in the tunnel, a dozen gray shadows scatter to safety. Let your attention drift just once and you're a rat pancake.

We get on the first car and Vin stretches his legs out on a row of seats. I sit across from him, looking down the car at the other passengers. Three girls together, laughing about who was getting checked out by who at the mall. Pretty girls, heavy on the makeup. Farther on, there's a guy with a receding hairline not reading the newspaper he's holding in front of him, eyeballing the girls instead. Definitely illegal thoughts sliming through his mind.

Will I know him when I see him? Or will I walk blindly past? Find the targeted women and find the psycho. Makes sense. Logical.

The leering guy with the paper just seems like your average creep.

On the ride out to Lawrence West Station, Vinny starts up again with his Schwarzenegger rant. Something about Arnie's bicep measurement back in his Mr. Olympia days.

I'm staring off into space when he says, "Are you even listening?"

"Huh? Yeah. Yeah. You know, I think this Arnold obsession might be a sign of latent homosexuality."

"Oh yeah?" he says, taking his left hand out of his pocket. "How many fingers am I holding up?"

It's an old joke, and one of the rare times he ever shows that hand. With the missing fingers, all he has to do is fold his thumb and index down to give a middle-finger salute. He's used it on everyone from classmates to teachers to cops. His secret weapon. When he gestures at teachers with the finger, they never call him on it—who's going to yell at the kid with the deformed hand? He can't help it. One time a cop said: "Are you pointing that at me?" And Vin explained how his hand was always like that, since the accident.

When we get off at Lawrence West, I tell him I have to go do something.

He shrugs. "I'll come with."

"Nah. You don't want to come. It's just something I have to do before I go home."

Vin gives me a suspicious look. "Like what?"

"Like nothing."

"You going to see a girl? Who?"

"No girl. Nothing. Don't worry about it." I can see his brain working overtime. "I'll tell you later. I gotta do it by myself."

"Is it illegal?"

Ever since I did community service, Vin thinks I'm a master criminal.

"Yeah, I'm going to knock off a bank. Now go. Call you tomorrow," I say, pushing him onto the escalator.

As he escalates, he calls down, "I'll want the full story. And pictures. And her name."

I shake my head, and he yells back at me all the way to the top, stumbling off when his feet hit the end of the escalator.

Her name. I don't have any names. Not real ones anyway; only the tags he gave them. I catch the next train for Wilson Station. At 10:40 a woman will be getting off there, a woman with red hair. Cherry.

You looked right at me on the subway today, but you didn't see me. Nobody sees me. Until it's too late. You always sit in the front car, in that little single seat near the driver. Do you feel safe there? Your hair is the color of rust. Is it your real color? Today your seat was taken by some snot with a skateboard. I wanted to snap his neck. But then you would have seen me, Cherry. And it's not time yet.

I refold the photocopy and stick it in my back pocket. He goes on like that for pages, endless ranting.

Down at the other end of the subway car, the single seat by the driver is empty. Across from me a construction worker dozes, his jeans white with plaster dust. Farther down, an old lady with a pinched face is reading *The National Enquirer*.

I check my watch: 10:30.

We stop at Yorkdale and a few shoppers fresh from closing time at the mall get on, loaded down with their bags.

The train doors are closing when a figure slips in, grabbing on to a pole as the subway starts up. She's breathing hard, been running to catch the train. Sliding into the single seat at the front, she tucks her red hair behind her ears and reaches for something in her bag.

My focus tunnels in on her, everything going gray and distant beyond the woman sitting in the single seat. I lean over a little to get a better view of her around a pole.

Oh my god. It's real—she's real. *This is really happening.* Up until now, the book was still just a book. I guess I didn't completely believe it. But this woman is living, breathing proof.

Now what do I do?

The wheels of the train squeal taking a turn, sending up a shower of sparks outside the window. I'm so stunned that she's here I forget to blink, afraid she'll vanish if I break my stare. Curly rust-red hair. Pale skin. Freckles. Dressed all in black. Just as she's described in the diary. She's wearing running shoes with her skirt and tights, like she just got off work and doesn't want to wear her heels home.

She pulls a Kit Kat out of her bag and starts eating it, like this is just another night, another ride home. Nothing to worry about.

Should I go over to her? And say what?

"Your life's in danger. There's this serial killer in training who's got his eye on you. Look at what he wrote in these pages here."

Of course she'd think I was a nut—that I was *the* nut with the thing for her, mapping out fantasies and planning our future. No. I'll wait and watch. See what happens. *He's* the one I have to find.

The stretch of track out to Wilson Station runs above-ground, crossing the 401 highway. It's completely dark out now. The red and white lights of the cars trail into the distance.

She finishes her Kit Kat and rolls the foil into a ball, looking out the window, or maybe at her own reflection.

There's nothing I can do that wouldn't make me look like a lunatic. No way to tell her. A wave of panic rushes over me when we pull into Wilson. The doubts shouting inside my head drown out anything useful.

The train stops and we exit at opposite ends of the car. I make like I'm checking my watch, waiting to see which way she'll go, which exit. It's 10:40. She's right on time, according to his notes.

Cherry walks past me, close enough for me to smell her perfume. Something flowery and a little sharp. I pause for a few beats, seeing if anyone else shows interest in her, another shadow on her tail.

Just me. Most of the passengers take the exit for the bus terminal. I tail her to the Wilson Avenue exit.

Does she live close by? Has the nut followed her home before? Is he waiting up there on the street?

There are no addresses listed for his targets in the diary. From his notes, that was his next step, scouting their neighborhoods. But the last entry is at least two weeks old by now. So how far has he gone? Losing the diary might have set him back a bit, but I'm sure he's got their schedules committed to memory.

I give her some distance so I'm not too obvious. A departing train drags a breeze down into the station, flipping the pages of a phone book deserted on the stairs, cooling the sweat on my forehead. On the sidewalk a busker is doing a bad imitation of Jimi Hendrix on his electric guitar, hooked up to a whiny amplifier. I spot Cherry hurrying by the noisemaker with her hands over her ears. Hanging back, I study the crowd for anyone suspicious. Cherry waits for the light at the corner and glances back, scowling at the guitarist. Under the harsh glare of the streetlights her pale skin looks ghost white. Her eyes shift and she catches me watching her.

Look away. Look away, I tell myself. My gaze darts to the guitarist, then back to the woman. To the street and back to her. I must look like one suspicious character, standing there at the top of the stairs.

First rule of surveillance you pick up from any cop show: see, but don't be seen. Well, that's blown.

The light goes green, and she crosses with the crowd. I trail behind with my head down. Trying to stick to the shadows, doing my best to stay out of range of the streetlights, I track her for a couple of blocks. She turns onto a side street where it's just her and me on the sidewalk. There's nobody that I can see watching from the other side of the street.

Are you here? Hiding in the dark under the trees, in the shadows between parked cars? Are you hunting tonight?

I'm sweating buckets now. The heat seems to rise from the baked pavement. Swiping at a drop that hangs on the tip of my nose, I watch the woman glance behind her to where I'm following half a block back. Instinctively I slow down, which I realize makes me even more suspicious.

Don't worry, I wish I could say. I'm here to save you.

Which would scare the crap out of her.

Cherry speeds up now, not breaking into a run or anything, but enough so I know I've spooked her. I stop and let her go, keeping an eye on her as she climbs the steps to a three-story apartment building. She fumbles for her keys, drops them, finally gets the door open, and rushes inside.

Damn! What the hell am I doing? I just terrified that woman—stalking her when I'm supposed to be protecting her. I'm doing what *Roach* does, except I'm sure he's way better at it.

I wipe my forehead dry on the sleeve of my T-shirt and turn back for the subway. I'm in way over my head.

Where was my plan? God knows *he's* got one. He's been training for this his whole life.

Me, I'm just the guy who found his book.

I've got to go back to the diary and study it like a Bible, find where he slips up and gives himself away.

There's got to be something.

TWELVE

When I get home it's a few ticks before midnight. Mom's up watching *Nightline*, where they're discussing a bloody coup someplace I've never heard of—one of those countries that keep changing their names. But a new name can't change who you are or where you've been.

"I missed your call," Mom says to me as I kick my shoes off.

Joining her on the couch, I squeeze my brain trying to remember what she's talking about. "What call?"

She's got that pissed-off stare, not looking at me on purpose. "Exactly. What call?"

Now I get her. "Oh, sorry, Mum. The time got away from me."

"I phoned around to your friends. Vinny told me you had a late date."

When Vin gets an idea in his head, you need a sledgehammer to knock it out.

"Wasn't really a date." I try to explain.

She turns to me with interrogator eyes. "Was there a girl?"

"Mmm. Yes."

"Were you alone with this girl?"

"Yes." Sort of.

"That's what they call a date, honey."

The interrogator softens now, giving me the once-over like she hasn't seen my face every day for the last seventeen years. Maybe she's checking for lipstick, hickeys, or crumpled condom wrappers sticking out of my pocket.

"Am I forgiven?" I ask.

She squinches her eyes in consideration. "Will you call next time?"

"I'll call, I'll fax, I'll e-mail—"

"Smart guy." She slaps my knee. "So, is she as smart as you?"

"Don't know."

"She pretty?"

"I guess." I didn't exactly spend my time with Cherry thinking about whether she was smart or pretty.

She waits for more, but when nothing comes, she shakes her head. "Well, don't go gushing all over the place about it. That's all I get? A grunt, a 'don't know,' an 'I guess'?"

I shrug. "I don't know. I guess."

A heavy sigh. Then she says, "Hungry?"

I didn't realize it till she asked, but I'm starving. "Sure."

"Grilled-cheese sandwich?"

"Maybe two?"

"My little piggie," she calls me, poking me in the stomach.

Surreal is the word for how things feel right now. I've

spent the last couple of hours fumbling around trying to find one particular psycho in a city that must have hundreds of them. And now, after a hard night of stalking, sweating, and confusion, I'm home eating Mom's grilled-cheese sandwiches, chatting about an imaginary date I was just on.

Later, somewhere between late-night talk shows, she nudges me awake. "Get to bed. You have to be up early tomorrow."

I think I'll sleep tonight, even with nothing settled—with some things even muddier than before. Some Chinese guy once said a thousand-mile journey begins with a single step. Well, my first step was kind of a stumble.

But it was a step.

THIRTEEN

Last fall, when I was dead to the world, sleepless and swallowed by guilt, Dad cornered me in my room.

I was sitting at my desk, staring at a history textbook. I'd read the same paragraph four times and still didn't know what it was about. Dad walked in and started wandering around.

"What's this?" he said, picking up a Stephen King Mom had bought for me weeks before.

"A book," I said.

"Any good?"

"I don't know."

He tossed it on top of the radiator, then went and sat on the foot of my bed. Dazed and confused was my natural state back then, so I was just kind of staring into space when Dad started waving his hand.

"Can I have your attention here?" he said.

"Yeah," I mumbled, using all my strength to pull things into focus. "What's going on?"

"What's going on is you're walking around like a zombie. I don't like it."

"Sorry," I said.

"Sorry does nothing," he told me.

There was a long silence. I waited, tapping my pen against the desktop while he picked at a Band-Aid on his thumb. He always had some kind of cut from work. When I was little, he'd tell me, "Those machines have teeth." And I thought that was for real, that they were actually taking bites out of him.

"I saw this thing on *Sixty Minutes* one time," he said. "About a secret service agent who was assigned to protect President Kennedy the day he got shot. He was riding on the running board of the follow-up car behind Kennedy's, keeping an eye on the crowd. When he heard the first shot, he thought it was just a firecracker. But then he saw the president lurch to the side and grab his neck. The second shot missed. The agent jumped from the follow-up car and ran to catch up to Kennedy. But there was no time. A couple seconds later the third shot hit the president in the head. He was down and dying by the time the agent jumped on the back of the car and started crawling toward him."

I had no idea what this story had to do with anything, so I just sat there waiting him out.

"You have to understand, this guy's whole job—his whole life—was about taking a bullet for the president. Anyway, so now it's fifteen years later and Mike Wallace is interviewing the agent on *Sixty Minutes*. And the guy's still a wreck. 'If only I'd been a second faster,' he says. 'If only I could have made it in time to take that third bullet.' The guy's just destroyed, shaking and weeping. And Mike's saying how there's no way he could have made it in time. It just wasn't humanly possible."

I rubbed the back of my neck, getting tired from focusing my attention for so long. In his clumsy way, Dad was trying to tell me something.

"So I'm watching this poor guy. Destroyed by guilt, really eaten up by it. Even though it was impossible for him to have done anything." Dad looked up at me. "And you know, I really got it."

He stood up and started pacing around behind me. It's a small room for all that agitated energy.

"I've been a guy a lot longer than you have," he said. "And I gotta tell you, it doesn't go away—that thing, the belief or whatever, that one day you're going to be a hero. All guys think that. It's bred into you. Every movie you ever see tells you that one day you'll get your chance. It doesn't go away, either. I'm still waiting for mine."

I could hear him behind me, cracking his knuckles one by one. "The thing is, you don't know if you could have saved that girl. She might have even pulled you down with her." He was quiet for a moment. "Tough to live with not knowing. But what choice have you got?"

I nodded, but it was obvious to both of us that this wasn't sinking in.

"I hear what you're saying," I said, hoping that would end the conversation.

"No, you don't," he sighed. "You're not hearing me."

I turned to glance over my shoulder at him, standing by the window, leaning his arm on the sill.

"Hear this," he said. "You're worrying your mother. Seeing you like this is really killing her."

I frowned. Why was he trying to make me feel even worse? Then it hit me what he was doing.

"You're trying to guilt me into not feeling guilty?" I said.

He nodded. "Something like that. Whatever works, kid."

Back when I got arrested for the B and E, the worst part wasn't Dad shouting at me over and over "What were you thinking? What were you thinking?" The worst part was the way Mom looked at me. Like she was looking at a ghost. Like she'd lost me. When we got home from the station, she came to me in my room. She didn't say anything. She just grabbed me and hugged me, held me tight. It was almost violent the way she did it, half knocking the wind out of me.

So Dad's Kennedy story didn't do it for me. The head doctor and the pills didn't do squat. But when I started to see how Mom was looking at me, that did it.

Wasn't quick, or easy. But I had to wipe that look from her eyes.

Guilt versus guilt.

Whatever works.

FOURTEEN

People in the Jungle dream of one thing on summer nights. They toss and turn, smothered by the heat. Lying limp in puddles of sweat, they dream of the cool relief of an ice-breathing air conditioner humming softly to them in the dark. Air conditioners are as rare as college diplomas in the Jungle.

When it gets so bad you think your toes are melting, that's when we head for the one place where winter still reigns in the heart of summer.

The Ignatius Howard Public Library, also known as the Igloo. The temperature in there stays at a constant deep freeze all summer—room temperature, if you live at the North Pole.

It wasn't my idea to bring Wayne. I had a bite after work and then called Vinny to come with me. I needed someone to talk to about all this stuff, and I figure he's got the kind of brain power I'm going to need to find my killer.

When we were heading out, Wayne was sitting in a lawn chair out front of B building, soaking his feet in a kiddie pool. "Hey. Where we going?" Wayne called out.

"Library," I told him. "You don't want to come."

I said that because I knew Wayne was going to bug us if he came. You can't take him anywhere. I mean, I like the guy—he's the brother I never wanted—but bring him to a library and you're asking for a riot.

"They have the Internet, don't they?" Wayne asked.

I groaned inside, and groaned outside in case Wayne wanted to take the hint. But he told us to wait, he was going to grab his shoes.

"Do we make a break for it?" Vin said.

"No good. He knows where we're going. There is no escape."

What you should know about Vinny and Wayne is that they're sort of friends by default. Me and Wayne have been hanging out since we used to eat dirt together in the sandbox in the park. Vin came along about five years ago and fell in with me. The way I figure it, Vinny's the brains of our operation, Wayne's the muscle, and I'm the soul—or maybe the lower intestine. Who knows?

Everybody's cranky in this heat. As we walk the four blocks to the Igloo, Vinny starts in on Wayne. "I think they have some comic books at the library," Vin says. "So you won't have to strain anything."

Wayne fakes a laugh. "You're killing me. Hey, did they ever make a comic about that dolphin? You know, the one in that movie? What was he called?"

They're like kids fighting in the backseat. "Play nice now," I tell them.

Wayne's not finished, though. "Was it . . . Flipper? Yeah, that's right, Flipper. Now where have I heard that name before?"

Vin's been trying to shake that name for five years. He tries his best to keep his hand out of sight, thinking people have to forget sometime. But a really nasty nickname never dies—it'll go on your gravestone.

So love is in the air between them, like the stink of hot tar, when we walk into the Igloo and feel that sweet frosty blast.

Wayne moans way too loud, saying "Oh yeah, baby, that's the stuff." Me and Vinny quickly separate ourselves from him and head for the stacks, while Wayne greets the woman on the desk with, "Hey, you got filters on the Internet computers here? Or can you look up anything?"

God knows what he's going to look up.

Vinny goes to check out the new fiction shelves. I stop at one of the library catalog computers and punch up the Subject category. So what do I type? Is there a listing for *psychos* or *nutcases*? I keep it simple and decide on murder. Which leads me to the true crime section.

When I see the size of the section, I have to wonder, who reads this stuff? I mean, suspense novels like *The Silence of the Lambs*, okay. But real blood-and-gore serial murder? Is that supposed to be entertainment?

Standing in front of the section is a fiftyish woman flipping through a book with photos that would give Charles Manson nightmares. She looks like a heavy smoker, gray hair, gray skin, yellow fingers. The book with the crime-scene pictures goes into the pile she's collecting. She looks like someone you'd expect to see at a bingo game, playing ten cards and arranging her Beanie Babies mascots for luck.

I scan the titles on the shelves. *Helter Skelter. The Hare Krishna Murders. The Stranger Beside Me.*

I don't know, it's not like I'm looking for a story to read. Thrills and chills and all that crap. I don't want a movie of the week.

Then one catches my eye. *Loving Death: Inside the Mind of the Serial Killer.* I read on the jacket that the author is a former FBI agent who tracked down these killers. That's what I need, a little guidance from a pro. I go find where Vinny's set up with a stack of fiction and graphic novels, over by the windows that let in the late-afternoon light. The Igloo's got these blue chairs you can really sink into, and I take the one next to Vin.

"Whatcha got?" he asks.

I show him the cover. "Murder book. What're you reading?"

"It's called *Watchmen.* A classic graphic novel. Real genius. Hot stuff."

Hot is one thing we're not. Now that we've been melting for the last month in the un-air-conditioned real world, the air in the Igloo tastes like it's been imported from the Himalayas. You almost expect to find frost lining the shelves. My brain's been limping through the heat wave, but this place gives me some focus, wakes me up. Which is what I need right now.

It doesn't take long to realize I've found what I'm looking for. This guy, Mason Lucas, was a profiler for the FBI's behavioral science unit. A psycho hunter. Cops and agents sent him notes and crime-scene photos from unsolved murders. Lucas went over all the evidence: autopsy reports, how the body was disposed of, and police interviews with family and friends of the victim. All the little gruesome details. Then he'd put together a profile of the unknown killer for the local cops.

It's pretty wild, the things he figured out about the killers just from notes and Polaroids. Lucas talks about how serial killers leave behind a kind of personality fingerprint when they murder someone. You are how you kill—that kind of thing.

Mason Lucas leads me through what goes into the making of serial killers. They usually come from broken families, having histories of abuse and neglect. As kids they felt powerless, with no control over anything in their lives. Which sounds like a lot of people to me, like some of my neighbors in the Jungle. But only the tiniest fraction of a fraction of these kids will grow up to kill people. These psychos are also pretty smart—not evil-genius Hannibal Lecter smart, but with a little higher than usual IQ's.

Then there's something profilers call the Homicidal Triad—three childhood behaviors that are shared by most serial killers. The Triad goes like this:

1) Cruelty to animals. These guys get off on torturing dogs, cats, and anything small and furry they can get their

hands on. It gives them a sense of power—life-and-death control over another creature.

2) Bed-wetting. That surprises me. Hard to picture these lean mean killing machines as former members of the rubber-sheet brigade. But this wetting the bed stuff ties in to their lack of control, and the frustration and shame they feel over it.

3) Fire-starting. Arson gives the young serial killer a rush, not just from the destruction of property, but from how he can manipulate so many people. Firefighters, cops, victims— whole crowds of men and women under his control.

This triad is all about power, and the warped ways these guys go around trying to obtain it.

The shiver that settles between my shoulder blades is only partly from the Igloo air. The guy in the diary, the roach, has shown at least two of these behaviors. The fires and the animals. He didn't share any news about his bed-wetting problem—probably wouldn't want to admit that kind of lack of control even to himself—but seeing all these indicators laid out in print confirms my fears. This is for real.

There's a sudden commotion a few rows over, shaking me from my thoughts. Out of sight from where we're sitting, I hear what must be the librarian saying, "You can't look that up here. That's disgusting."

"What? I'm, like, doing research." It's Wayne's voice, and when I look over to Vinny, he just rolls his eyes to the ceiling. Wayne is being Wayne. Can't take him anywhere.

"You're going to have to leave now," the disgusted woman tells him.

"Hey, what about freedom of speech?"

Wayne appears, walking down the aisle with the librarian's hand on his shoulder guiding him to the exit. I don't know if libraries have bouncers, but she's definitely got the build for one. She has the shoulders of a linebacker.

"Come on." Wayne tries to shrug her off. "I'll be good. I'm with those guys," he adds, pointing in our direction. As if that's going to help him.

The woman pauses a second, looking over to where we're sitting.

Vinny shakes his head. And I say, "I've never seen this guy before."

Wayne gets dragged off toward the doors. The last thing I hear before he's bounced is: "Man, I'm gonna sue."

And then the cool silence falls again.

"Well, that didn't take long," Vinny says. "I think he's got ADD."

"*Add?*"

"Attention deficit disorder," Vin informs me.

I grunt. "All I know is he's a P.E.R.V."

Someone knocks on the window behind our chairs. Wayne gestures us to come out, mouthing "Let's go."

I grab one of those little midget pencils you always find in libraries and scrawl a note on a slip of paper: WE'RE STAYING WHERE IT'S COOL! I think for a second, then add SUCKER at the end. Holding it up against the window, I watch Wayne read the note, and I swear I can see his lips moving. Then he leans in, pressing his nose against the glass to make a pig face, at the same time giving us the finger— actually a double finger, both hands up against the window. Wayne holds the pose for a second, then pushes off and walks away.

After the excitement, I go back to my book. The FBI guy talks about how serial killers grow up. He says they learn from their own abusive situations how to dominate and control a weaker person. It's like they're in training all their lives. Getting a feeling of power from the torture of small animals, they escalate to bigger things. A lot of them move from abusing pets to fire-starting, where they can finally control and manipulate people. Until they find that even this power isn't enough. It's like my Roach realizing that his experiments in fire and torture are just "kids' stuff."

Mason Lucas has a name for this "escalation of increasingly destructive aberrant behavior," this demented growth pattern moving from pets to fires to people.

He calls it acceleration.

"So how's your murder book?" Vinny asks, breaking into my reading. "Is it the feel-good story of the year?"

"This is mind-blowing stuff," I tell him.

"I thought you only read Stephen King and sci-fi."

"Yeah, but I'm not really reading this for fun," I say.

I'm dying to tell somebody what's going on. And Vin is

the only somebody on the planet who might get what I'm trying to do.

"Let me ask you a hypothetical question," I say.

"Hype away."

"Suppose you knew somebody was going to be killed?"

"What, am I getting psychic visions?" Vin cracks.

"Suppose you found the killer's plans, like written down somewhere."

"What, like: 'Dear diary. I think I'll whack the pizza delivery guy. He forgot the garlic bread again.'"

"Be serious. Make an effort," I tell him.

"Oh, serious. Right. I don't know. I'd give his secret plans to the cops. They'd pick him up. End of story."

"And what if you couldn't go to the cops?"

"Why not?" Vin asks.

"Lots of reasons. Maybe they wouldn't take it seriously. They're busy solving real crimes. They'd just think it was made up or something. And it's not like the guy who wrote it signed his name and address."

Vin shrugs. "I give up, Batman, what do I do?"

"You try and catch the killer yourself," I say.

"With what? My Swiss Army knife and my library card?"

"You know, for a sidekick, you're not very supportive."

"I always thought *you* were the sidekick," he says. "What's this supposed to be about, anyway? Is this from a movie or something?"

Now I pull out a wad of folded pages from my back

pocket, photocopies I made of some diary pages. Flattening them out, I hand them over. Vinny gives me a look like he thinks I've been smoking some seriously mind-pretzeling substances, but he tosses his book on the table and takes up the copies. The top one has writing scrawled around a Polaroid of a dead cat hanging from its neck on a length of chain.

"What's this, your new hobby? It's . . ." His voice trails off halfway through the remark.

Holding the pages closer to make out the writing, he finishes one and moves on to the next. No wisecracks from him now as he reads. I ran off a handful of pages from the diary, not wanting to carry the book around with me. It's hidden in my closet behind a pile of old hockey equipment, like a stack of *Playboys* I don't want Mom to find.

"Is this from one of those true-crime books?" Vinny asks.

"It's from some kind of diary that showed up in the lost and found. I was looking for a book to read and saw this."

"No way."

"Yeah. Seriously. Look at the last page."

He shuffles to the page that lists the killer's targets.

"You've got to turn this in," he tells me.

I shake my head. "Who knows if they'd even believe it? They're not going to waste time on a crime that hasn't happened, that might never happen. Besides, my prints are all over that thing, and they've already got those on file from that B and E I did with Wayne. They might even think I just made it up myself."

"Do you know what graphology is?" Vinny asks out of nowhere.

"Sure. It's the . . . ology of graphs."

He sighs. "It's the study of handwriting. All they'd have to do is compare a sample of your writing to this and they'd see it wasn't you who wrote it."

"I don't know."

"I know! You gotta turn this in."

"But maybe I found this diary for a reason. Maybe I'm supposed to find this guy myself."

"Okay . . . ," Vin says, giving me a look. "That's definitely crazy. This is some serious crap here. If this is right, then a woman's going to die."

I take the pages back from him. "I know," I say. "I know."

Vinny's right, of course. He's like the voice of sanity. But damn, it's hard to give this up.

"So?" he says.

I slouch back into the cushions. "So I gotta turn it in."

FIFTEEN

I told Jacob I had to get off early for a doctor's appointment.

"Make sure you clock out, then," he said.

Like it's a major felony if I rip off the city for a couple hours of minimum wage.

"And keep whatever you've got to yourself," he added.

As if I was going to sneeze and turn the lost and found into a hot zone.

I chose the fifty-second division downtown, because it's on the other side of the city from the twelfth, where I got arrested with Wayne. I'm being a little paranoid; I'm not exactly public enemy number one. But if they recognized me—who's going to believe a guy who tried to steal a toilet?

The rank smell of the fifty-second hits me as I step through the doors. Stale sweat smothered with pine air freshener. My already queasy stomach does a back flip.

If there's an air conditioner in this building, it must be on its last legs. The place is like an oven. My heart's gunning, and my sweat-drenched shirt sticks to me like plastic wrap.

I make way for a couple of cops heading for the door.

Turn and run, my brain's screaming at me. But instead, I force myself to step up to the counter that stretches half the length of the room. There seems to be only one cop on the desk, a middle-aged black woman talking to a red-faced old man.

"You can't post bail until he's been arraigned," she says.

"I just want to take him home."

"I understand. But see, your grandson isn't even here in this building. He's down at central holding. Here." She grabs a slip of paper and writes something on it. "This is where you have to go."

"Can't I just take him home?" he says.

She hands him the slip and he studies it like it's written in hieroglyphics.

"Next," she calls out.

I glance around at the half-full benches that face the desk. Nobody stirs from their seats. They must be waiting for something else.

"I need some relief from this heat," a drunken voice shouts out from the benches.

"And I need you to shut up now, Clarence," she tells him. "You can sit there till the detective is ready to see you. If you start mouthing off, your butt's on the street."

Clarence grumbles, but his mouth stays shut.

"Next," she says.

I step up. "I need to talk to somebody."

She picks up a miniature fan from the desktop and holds it in front of her face. Her eyes have the glazed look of someone who's been lied to all day long. "I'm somebody. Go ahead."

"I guess I want to report something."

She squints at me through the little draft the fan's stirring up.

I reach into the Safeway bag I'm carrying and take out the diary. My palms are slick against its smooth cover.

"I think someone's going to get hurt. Maybe even killed."

"Yeah?" she says. "Who?"

"I don't know who exactly. See, I found this diary. I'm working at the transit lost and found, and this got turned in."

I set the book down on her desk, reluctantly letting it go. I don't know what I was expecting—I mean, I didn't think they were going to immediately call in a SWAT team—but it would help if she was actually paying attention.

Instead, she's focused on the old man who wants to take his grandson home. He's counting out money from his wallet onto the counter.

"Sir, what are you doing?"

He looks up, confused. "I—I've got the bail money here. But now I lost count. . . ." He trails off, mumbling.

"Okay, you have to listen to me now," she says. "Put your money away. Grab a seat, and I'll get somebody to run you over to central holding. Sit. Over there."

She points him to the benches.

"Good. Now you stay there," she tells him when he finds a spot.

Then she turns back to me. "Okay. So what's in this book?"

"Well, it's like a diary. This guy's been stalking women. He's a real nut—gets off on killing animals and setting fires. And I think maybe he's going to kill someone."

"What's his name?" the cop asks.

"I don't know. He doesn't say what his name is."

She lets out a gusty sigh and uses her pen to flip open the diary. She turns a few pages, her face expressionless.

"You make up this scrapbook all by yourself?"

"What? No. It's not mine. I just found it."

I knew this would happen. And I'm sure I look nervous and guilty as hell.

"So what do you want me to do with this?" she asks, flipping it shut.

"I thought you could . . . uh, find out who wrote it."

"No name. No address. A few clippings anybody could have cut out of the paper."

"You could get fingerprints off it, right?"

"Right. Listen here, you don't seem like a bad kid. But maybe you should find a better way to spend your summer vacation."

I'm stunned. I'm speechless. I don't know what I expected, but nothing like this. She doesn't believe me, doesn't believe the diary.

"You're not even going to take it?" I ask.

Those glazed eyes stare back at me for a long second.

A man in a sports jacket comes down the stairs to the right, at the end of the desk. Glancing over at the benches, he says, "Clarence, what do you got for me? Better be good."

"Jack." The desk cop calls him over. "Can I borrow you for a second?"

Jack comes over on my side of the counter, giving me the cop stare that drills right into me. Sweat trickles down my back.

"My turn," Clarence whines, standing by the benches. "Supposed to be my turn now."

"Did you take a number?" Jack asks the drunken man.

"Didn't know there were any numbers," Clarence says.

"There aren't," says Jack. "So you get your turn when I say you get it. Got it?" Then he turns to the desk cop. "What's up?"

"We've got a guy here says he found this diary, says it's written by a crazy man who's out to hurt somebody."

"That right?" he says, standing a little too close. He's got a few inches on me and I instinctively move back a step. "A crazy man's diary?"

The phone rings and the desk cop answers it.

"Well, yeah," I say. "I mean, I don't know how crazy he really is, but I think he's out to hurt someone."

Jack reaches over and picks up the book. Leaning against the counter, he flips through it, stopping for a moment to squint at Roach's scribbled handwriting, then moving on past the newspaper clippings and some crude drawings of naked women.

If you just skim the diary you don't get the same impact as if you study it and follow how Roach's mind works. If you

only glance at the pages, it looks like nothing but a big mess. It takes time to see past that.

Jack snaps the book shut and sets it on the counter. "You know how many seriously deranged people we've got in the greater metropolitan area?" he asks me.

I shrug, shaking my head.

"Upwards of fifty thousand. And a lot of them like to scribble down the diarrhea that runs through their brains."

"Yeah. But this is serious. I mean—"

"Can I use the bathroom?" Clarence calls out, holding up his hand like a little kid in a classroom.

Jack ignores him, scratching at a drop of sweat that runs down his left temple.

"I really gotta go," Clarence pleads.

"Should I leave this with you?" I ask. "Can you look into it?"

"Yeah. Sure." Jack shoots an irritated look at the desk cop that says, Why did you bring me into this? "We'll put the whole squad on it," he tells me. "Just leave it here."

Then he turns away and points at the drunken man. "You got some information for me, Clarence? Let's do it."

Jack leads him up the stairs.

The desk cop finishes up on the phone.

"So?" she says to me now, hanging up.

"I guess I should leave it with you?"

"Right." She shifts the diary over with her pen and sets her fan beside it. "Leave your name and number and we'll get back to you."

She pushes a slip of paper over to me but doesn't give

me a pen. Yeah, they'll get back to me. How about never?

"Next," she calls out.

I stand there dazed, trying to think of anything I can say to convince her. Make her believe.

Then she gets up from her chair behind the desk. "Hey, Matthew," she says to a passing cop. "Wait up."

She walks to the end of the counter. "Can you run the old man there down to holding? He's got to bail out his grandson."

"What am I, a cabbie now?" the other cop says.

I'm still standing here, paralyzed. They're going to file this thing in a drawer somewhere. This is what I told Vinny would happen. Absolutely nothing. A dead end.

I can't just let this thing gather dust while Roach is out there hunting every night.

I glance at the diary, then over at the two cops. And with my eyes on them, I reach up and grab the book. Then, as calmly as I can with my heart seizing up, I walk toward the doors.

They're still arguing about giving the old man a ride when I step outside. Street noise crashes down on me. Expecting a hand on my shoulder any second, I rush down the sidewalk with enough adrenaline pumping through me to outrace a cheetah.

SIXTEEN

There are a lot of passages where Roach writes about the "old bitch." At first I thought it was his mother he was talking about, but a couple of times he slips up and calls her Gran. Here's what he says about his grandmother:

I know what it's like to be a mouse, with no key to the cage. When I was 12, the old bitch put a lock on the door to my basement room. Every night she'd lock me in. Said she knew what filth boys got into. "Rape on the brain," she said. Like I was going to come after her or something. Some mornings she'd forget about me down here. I'd scream at the crack under the door, beat my knuckles raw on the wood. But that's useless. She's near stone deaf. I made plans to kill her. So many ways. I'd picture her face, how it would look when she saw it coming. But she's an old witch and she's got power in her. Five feet nothing, a rack of bones, I could break her so easy. But she's like the creature in that movie Alien—you cut it and it bleeds acid, burns a hole right through you. Last week she cut her finger sweeping up a broken glass. I was shocked to see how red her blood was, just plain human red. I expected something blue, like antifreeze, to come pouring out. But it was red like mine. Like the blood I spilled the night I finally broke the lock on my cage. I'd been working on it awhile, bruising the crap out of my shoulder, throwing my weight against the wood at night until it finally gave way. The whole doorjamb splintered and I gashed my arm on a screw. Lying there on the floor slippery with my blood, I felt like I was born again.

SEVENTEEN

I meet up with Vinny in a little downtown park. Calling it a park is being generous. It's more like a putting green with a few trees and a small fountain.

I spot him leaning against a tree.

"Hey, Duncan. I'm starving. You buying?"

"Yeah, I'll add it to your tab."

Parked on the street nearby is a fast-food truck with FRANCO'S LUNCHOPOLIS painted on the side. We go and grab some pizza slices and Cokes.

"You're a cheap date," Vin tells me. "There's no way you're getting to third base on a slice."

I point to a sliver of shade under a tree. We go sit and eat. I use my napkin to soak up the grease off my slice.

"This isn't a meal, it's a death wish," I say. "Should come with a defibrillator."

Vinny shrugs. "Live fast. Eat junk. Leave a bloated corpse."

I glance over at the fountain, where a blond girl runs

squealing through the ankle-deep water. Her skinny little arms are burning pink in the sun.

"So, how long's your lunch?" Vinny says.

"An hour."

"Why did you call me down here?" he asks. Then in mock panic he says: "We're not breaking up, are we?"

I smile and swig some Coke.

"Remember back a few months, I told you about those dreams I was having?"

"The ones about Jennifer Lopez?" he says.

I wipe the moisture from the sweaty pop can off on my jeans. "The ones about the girl who drowned."

Vin groans. "Why do you have to talk about that? Can't you just let it fade?"

"They started up again."

"Why?"

I don't answer, watching the girl in the fountain pick up the change people have tossed in. There's a moment of silence as Vinny pulls a long string of cheese off his slice and feeds it into his mouth.

"That girl," he says, swallowing. "She went out too deep, got a cramp or whatever, and went under. It sucks. It's tragic. But it's not on you, man. You can't save the world. Gotta get that idea out of your head. That's why Kimmy dumped you. You couldn't let it go."

"Thanks for reminding me."

"What's that in the bag?" Vin asks, his voice sounding a little funny, like he already knows what's in there.

I take the diary out and set it on the grass between us.

"I thought we agreed you were going to turn that in," he says.

"I tried."

"How do you *try*? You just hand it to them, and then it's their problem."

"I showed it to these cops down at the fifty-second division, told them what it was and everything."

"And?"

"And . . . I don't know. They didn't believe me, or didn't care. They thought I was pulling something, or they didn't think it was real. But this one cop just left it lying there on the counter while she went and helped somebody else. Anybody could have picked it up and walked off."

"So what are you going to do with it now?"

"I know it sounds crazy, but I think maybe there's a reason I found it."

"Not that again," he says, shaking his head at me.

"Look, maybe if we track this guy down, then we'll have something to take to the cops. Something they'll pay attention to."

" 'We'? Did I hear 'we'?"

"The way I see it, I've got the looks, but you've got the brains. I'll make a deal with you—we locate this sick nut and then we turn the diary over to the cops. It's not like I'm saying we have to take him down ourselves."

Vinny closes his eyes and holds his cold Coke against his forehead. He lets out a long breath.

"This is all about that drowned girl, isn't it," he says quietly. "You think because you couldn't save her—you're getting, what, a second chance?"

I wipe my greasy hands off on the grass.

"I need this," I say, knowing how weird that sounds.

In the fountain, the girl is still splashing away, looking impossibly happy with the handful of change she's found.

I tell Vin a little bit of what happened to me at the pool, how I freaked out, what I saw.

"I just need to *do* something," I say.

He's quiet for the longest time.

"Okay," he says finally. "But man, I hope you're right about this."

EIGHTEEN

Strange dream. I find myself underwater, and all around it's dead black. I could be blind, it's so dark. My skin tightens against the touch of the cold water surrounding me. I'm sinking slowly into a big nothing. But I'm not scared. I can breathe even though I'm submerged, like I belong down here, like this is where I live. I was born to swim.

There's a low buzz coming through the dark, like the sound motorboats make when you hear them underwater. It grows louder the farther I sink. Maybe the boat's getting closer, going to pass by way up above. But the sound, when I focus on it, isn't coming from the surface. It's rising from below me, down where I'm headed. I drift deeper and deeper.

There's a blue light emerging now from the blackness. I watch it take shape with the dumb fascination I get in dreams sometimes, when I see something I recognize but can't put a word to it.

The buzz gets louder, and now I can see my hands and legs in the murky light. I hit bottom with a jolt, falling to my knees. As I get up, the thick muck sucks at my hands and feet, like it wants to pull me even deeper.

Now I see the source of the light. *Subway*—the word finally comes to me. The blue glow is coming from inside a subway car, sunk down here at the bottom.

I swim over, and finding an open door, I go inside. The pole I grab on to is slick with mossy seaweed. The fluorescent lights overhead sputter, making shadows dance down the length of the car. In the flickering, I see a figure up ahead, in that single seat beside the driver's compartment. Everything is blue in the glow. Her head is down, her long hair suspended above her and moving with the slight current.

I know her. I don't need to see the face. I remember it blushing a pale limp blue on that scorching day last summer, pulled from the deep water of Lake Ontario. But somehow she's still down here. Like this is where she lives. Like me.

Moving from pole to slippery pole, I pull myself along until I'm hanging in front of her.

"I'm sorry," I try to say, but the words have no sound, swallowed by the water. So I can only float there before her bowed head, giving her mute *Sorry's*.

The current shifts, brushing a freezing draft of water against me. Looking down the blue-lit car, I see a shadow step in through the open doors at the other end. Even in the fluorescent glow the dark figure shows no features. It eats the light. The shadow doesn't swim but walks toward us as if the underwater rules of floating and suspension don't apply to it.

The sudden freeze in the water only adds to my panic at the sight of this thing coming for us. Reaching out, I touch the hand resting in the girl's lap. It feels soft, boneless. Her eyes peer up at me through the floating hair—eyes without hope.

"We have to go." I mouth the words, gesturing with my head to the nearest doors.

"Not my stop," I read on her lips.

As the shadow grows closer, the temperature drops, and the water pressure here at the bottom triples in a second, squeezing my chest, making every breath an effort. With the cold sinking into my bones, and the ink-black form moving closer to take possession of the girl, I lunge at her, grabbing a limp arm to pull her out of her seat and drag her to safety. But the arm feels like it's made of rubber. Slippery as a fish, it escapes my hand.

"He's going to kill you!" I try shouting, as if the volume will make the words get through the liquid any easier. But her head bows even lower.

The pressure becomes a cold fist wrapped around my chest. When I look away from her, I see the shadow has stopped an arm's length away.

Too late. Always too late.

"Who are you?" I try to shout with what might be my last breath.

The black head studies me with its eyeless face, like it's wondering what kind of creature it's found here at the bottom. With one hand it makes a shooing motion at me, as if I'm an insect. The force of that little gesture throws me back through the water with the impact of a tidal wave into the end door that would connect to the next car if there was one.

Paralyzed by the water pressure, I'm forced to watch as the shadow reaches out to lift the girl's head. Her eyes are on me now, waiting for the pain. The ink-black fingers run over her mouth, and then one hand grips her lower lip while the other holds the upper.

And with one quick motion the hands pull apart, peeling her face off. Fast, like he's gutting a fish.

I wake with vomit rising in my throat. Jumping up in bed, my whole body clenched with panic, I clamp one hand over my mouth and fight with all my strength to force the bile back down. It must be a full minute before I breathe again, acid burning in my throat.

I'm freezing and sweating, weak from sleep but riding a fading rush of adrenaline. Stumbling over to the window, I lean there, sucking in the humid night air. I have to hold myself up on the window ledge, my legs are shivering so bad.

I can't stop seeing her, those eyes watching me even after her face is gone.

I can't do this! Can't do this anymore! There's no way I'm going to find him.

The night sky is gray with reflected city light. The stars

are lost in the haze. In the distance, I can pick out the lights from other apartments where people are spending a sleepless night. Two and a half million people in the city of Toronto. And one psycho hunting.

There's just no way.

NINETEEN

I have no idea what I'm going to say, but I dial the number anyway. I get Kim's voice mail.

"You got something to say?" her recording goes. "Well, it better be good." She dissolves into laughter at the end. Then comes the beep.

God, I hate these things. Talking to dead air.

"Hey, Kim. It's me. Duncan—in case you've forgotten the sound of my voice."

No. That's no good. Sounds way too bitter. After a couple of seconds of silence there's a beep and a computer voice says: "Press one if you're satisfied with your message. Press two if you want to re-record your message."

I hit two. "Message erased. Please re-record your message."

I wish it was as easy to go back and erase a few more things I've said to her.

Beep.

"Hi, Kim. It's Duncan. I was just thinking of you. And, um, wanted to see if you're okay. I know—same old me, trying to keep you out of danger. Anyway, I'm doing good.

Well, maybe not so good. Maybe really bad. But that's not why I'm calling. I only wanted to hear your voice. It's like . . . remember that thing you told me from Winnie-the-Pooh, you know, where Pooh reaches out and pokes Piglet and Piglet says, 'Why did you do that?' And Pooh says, 'I just wanted to be sure of you.' Which is why I'm calling, I guess. To poke you."

I don't know what else to say. The machine cuts me off anyway, giving me my options.

I try to picture her listening to this. I can't see it doing any good. What's changed? I'm still a basket case. She's still out there, taking risks, living her life.

I press two.

Message erased.

TWENTY

Before last week, my job seemed like a major waste of time. Today, with a clock ticking down somewhere, with a life ticking down, the job is agony. Right now, in the tunnels above my head, *he* might be riding the subway, hunting for the perfect girl to be his first victim.

Roach even has his own secret recipe for something like chloroform to knock them out. Following his script, he'll grab them off the street at night, load them in the backseat of his grandmother's old car, and drive them home.

Once he's done with his prep work, getting their schedules down and scouting their neighborhoods, he'll set his trap.

And here I am packing junk for the YMCA sale.

Jacob, who doesn't really care if I'm breathing so long as I'm on time to do the running, spoke more than a syllable to me today.

"Boxes have to be full and ready for noon Thursday," he said. That was my morning hello from him.

"Why noon?" I asked—not because I care, but if we're

going to be locked up together for the next month and a half, it might be good to crack the ice that runs in his veins.

"Noon's when the truck comes to haul this debris over to the Y," he said, then went back to his paper.

I filled a cup at the cooler. "So you been down here long?" I asked.

Jacob frowned, glancing up at the clock.

"I mean working here in the lost and found?" I added.

"Three years."

"Doesn't bother you? No windows, no air, no sun?"

He sniffed but didn't brush me off, actually thought for a second. "Who needs a window? What's there to see?"

"I don't know, anything. A tree maybe?"

"I'm going to sit and stare at a tree all day?"

"Some sun," I tried. "Air. Some fresh air would be nice."

He scratched one hairy ear, like my talking was irritating it. "Sun gives you cancer. And fresh air or stale air, it all breathes the same."

I don't know why I even tried. I folded the paper cup in my hand and tossed it in the trash. "I'll get started on those boxes."

And that's where I am now, checking a thousand little Post-it notes for expiration dates. Here's a baseball cap with a fake turd glued to the visor, and the slogan IT HAPPENS. How could someone leave this behind? Must be a family heirloom. That and the cap from Hooters, which has something else sticking up from its visor.

The one thing keeping me from cracking is that now I've

got Vinny on the case with me. We checked out a stack of true-crime books yesterday, and it's his job to read them and find something useful. He's kind of a speed reader, and he's got tons of free time.

Don't think about time, I tell myself. Because no matter how many books we read, it's still running out.

The phone rings up front.

Using my pen, I hold up some extra-large thong under-wear. We're talking a King Kong thong. Wondering how you lose your underwear on public transit, a mystery for the ages, I have to break away from the Kong thong when Jacob dings for me. I drop the underwear in the garbage and make a mental note to burn the pen.

When I get to the counter, Jacob grunts and gestures to the phone. I pick it up.

"Hello?"

"Hey, Duncan, it's me."

"Vinny. How'd you get this number?"

Down the counter, Jacob turns up his radio to drown me out.

"It's not like you're working in the Pentagon. I just looked it up."

"So what's going on?"

"I've been doing some research on that, um, problem we were talking about."

"Vin, this phone isn't bugged. You can talk normal."

Jacob edges the volume up some more. I stick a finger in my ear.

"My mom's in the next room," Vinny explains.

"Ah. How about we meet after I get off work?"

The old fart squeezes another few decibels out of his little radio. I scowl over at him.

"Where?" Vinny says.

We're having fries and shakes under an umbrella table outside the Barn. Vinny's filling me in on what he's found out.

"The FBI profilers say serial killers, you know, when they're starting out, aren't real sophisticated. Their first murders are done on impulse, not thought out all the way. And . . ." He pauses to chew a fry. "They're done close to home."

"How does that help?" I ask. "I can't just wait till he offs one of these women to track him down."

A lot of what the books talk about deals with using crime-scene evidence and the state of the corpse to profile the killer. Right now, there *is* no crime scene. And I want to keep it that way.

"Yeah," Vinny says. "But look at the pets he tortured, and the fires. Those are like his warm-ups for the big show. They cover a span of about ten years. The earliest ones would have been done close to home, in what the pros call the comfort zone."

"Okay. So?"

"So we've got the newspaper clippings from his little scrapbook."

I pull the straw from my shake and lick it clean, thinking. Then I use it to point at Vinny.

"What about those cats he killed and strung up? Did they give addresses where that happened?"

"They name a few streets up in Wilson Heights," Vin says. "There was a string of animal mutilations in the same area during the same time period. Busy guy."

Somewhere close by a heat bug starts up its electric whine. I stir my shake, staring off down the street to where the heat rising from the tar makes the air all wavy.

"And we've also got the diary entries about the fires he set," Vinny says. "He kept all the details: dates, addresses. Everything."

"How close do you think that'll get us to him?"

"Hopefully we can narrow him down to a few blocks. Maybe a neighborhood."

"Mr. Psycho's neighborhood," I say. "Where exactly does that get us, though? I mean, we can't really go canvassing house to house."

"Hey, man. Baby steps. I've only been working on this a day and a half. This is some crazy crap, eh?"

"Yeah. A big steaming pile of it," I say.

"Me and you going after this guy—it's like the Hardy Boys meet Hannibal Lecter."

Wayne walks up to our table, off work now and out of uniform.

"Right," I tell Vin. "Just so long as I'm the Hardy who gets to do the forbidden dance with Nancy Drew."

Wayne grabs a seat with us. "The only dance you'll be doing is the one-handed mambo." He pulls a wad of Dairy Barn scratch-and-win tickets out of his pocket.

"Start scratching, boys," he tells us. "We're going to be millionaires. Get me out of this grease pit."

We start scratching.

"Come on, new car," Vin says to his ticket.

"Come on, new life," Wayne tells his.

TWENTY-ONE

Roach doesn't write about his mother much. But when he gets on the subject—watch out! Raving lunatic.

SHE phoned this morning. I had to answer it, because even with the ringer set on high Gran couldn't hear it. The receiver's volume was maxed out too, so when I heard HER voice it spiked right through my eardrum. "Is that you, kid?" SHE said. I dropped the phone and yelled at the old bitch to deal with it.

I went down in the basement. But the walls in this place are like cardboard and Gran's a screamer. "What? What? I'm not sending you money! You're a whore, go do what whores do to make money."

Turned the radio on. Loud. Tried to kill the sound of HER voice in my head, but it got past all the noise. Squeezed my eyes shut and covered my ears. But SHE got in, always does. And I see HER now, when she'd come home painted like a clown, bringing back johns. At first I hated those perverts and the things they made her do. But they were nothing but dumb dogs running wild in the street. SHE's the one who dragged them back here, let them do any disgusting thing they wanted. SHE's the one who sent me hiding when they told her to lose the kid. . . .

It's all frantic scribbling after that, and I can only make out a few words.

I need a break. My brain is fried.

The sun set hours ago, but the heat sticks in the air. Even my eyelids are sweating. Somewhere in the Jungle, TV's are playing late-night talk shows, but the sounds of laughter and applause are muffled. Even the throbbing beat of acid rock from the nightly rave over in D building is subdued tonight. Everything seems stunned.

But me, I'm bouncing off the walls trying to figure my way deeper into Roach's world. There's got to be a key somewhere in these pages. But when I've read the same sick passage for the third time without getting anything new out of it, I know it's time to quit for the night.

I close the diary and stash it under my old hockey equipment.

Out in the living room, Mom's watching a *late* late movie. She's got two big box fans set up so she's being blown from all directions.

"Can't sleep?" she says.

I shake my head. "You?"

"No. I need the snoring beast beside me, or the quiet wakes me up."

I go into the kitchen and grab a Popsicle from the freezer. While I'm there, I stick my head in for a chilly blast, resting my cheek on a bag of frozen peas.

"Hey, make room for me in there," Mom says.

I pull out, the back of my head scraping a delicious dusting of frost onto the back of my neck.

She gets a Popsicle for herself. "Come watch the movie with me. It's set in Russia during the winter."

"Sounds like heaven," I say.

On the TV, a train with a plow attached to the front chugs through an endless snowbound landscape. It must be thirty below.

"So who's this Doctor Zavoogoo again?" I ask.

"Doctor Zhivago. He's a surgeon and a poet, caught up in the horrors of the Russian revolution."

"Okay. Whatever," I say. "I'm just in this for the weather." I rest my feet on the coffee table, nudging Mom's pile of books over a bit.

On the screen, a horse-drawn sled is speeding across a winter wonderland. Two figures swallowed up in furs huddle in back.

"Oh, this is my favorite part. The ice house."

The doctor and his beloved Lara have traveled to his old summerhouse in the country. But the place is seriously wrecked, windows shattered, the roof caving in. No way he's getting the damage deposit back.

Everything's covered in ice. Frost hides under the furniture like dust, with snow carpeting the floors.

As I sprawl on the couch, my bare leg rests against Mom's. The body heat bugs me and I pull away.

The doctor shivers as an arctic breeze gusts through the ice house, blowing snow off the drifts in the dining room.

"It's kind of a fixer-upper," Mom says.

"Who cares. When do we move in?"

TWENTY-TWO

"Man, if you keep this up," I tell Vinny, "I'm going to promote you from sidekick to full partner."

We're sitting at a booth in the Barn. Vin's flattening out a map of the city on the table, pushing the napkin dispenser out of the way. He's got it folded to show a certain section of north Toronto. Red and green marker dots are clustered in the Wilson Heights area.

"How did you do all this?" I ask.

"On the microfiche at the library. Old newspapers are not on the Net. And there was no index for the kind of thing we're looking for, no way to narrow the search. I had to go through years of *Crimewatch* sections to dig this all up."

He gives me his "You owe me" look—the same look I got last year when he wrote a book report for me on *The Sun Also Rises*.

"Okay," I say. "I'm impressed already. You the man! Now what's with the colored dots?"

"The red dots are for older incidents—animal mutilations and fires—the oldest going back about ten years.

Green is for newer ones, anything in the past five years."

"What about the yellow dot there?"

"That's just some mustard," Vin says. "I got hungry. Anyhow, most of the old ones are animal mutilations, with a few of what were probably his first fires in red too."

There must be almost thirty dots on the map. Roach has been busy. It's like he's in training, racing from one to two to three on the Homicidal Triad.

"Not bad, Vin."

"Not bad?" Vin leans back on his side of the booth, offended. "How about amazing? How about genius? You know, I didn't see you over at the Igloo, slaving away on the microfiche. I'm doing a lot of legwork here."

"I know. I know. Here comes some payback now."

Wayne walks over with our orders on a tray. I hurry to refold the map before he sees it. "Ladies," he says, sliding into the booth to join us. "You know, I wouldn't be insulted if you left a tip."

"Here's a tip," Vinny says. "Try doing some laundry."

Wayne's uniform looks like it's been deep fried.

"Doesn't the management say anything?" I ask.

He shrugs. "They've got me working in the back mostly now. And doing cleanup. The glamour jobs."

Wayne slouches in the seat beside me, watching us dig in to our burgers. Well, at least I dig in. Vinny always eats like he's performing an autopsy, examining each bite for evidence or something.

"They really put sawdust in these for filler?" Vin asks.

"We like to call it our secret formula. Nothing wrong with sawdust. It's good fiber." Wayne stretches and groans. "I can't take much more of this. The smell of those burgers—it's like monkey dung."

"Which I hear is also used as filler," I say.

"Good fiber," Vin adds, examining his burger between bites.

"Remember Brenda Hall, from school?" Wayne asks. "You know, with the serious curves? Anyway, I always got a good vibe off her, like she was open to me asking her out. So she comes in yesterday, and I'm chatting her up real nice. And I get nothing off her. It's like she was embarrassed I was even talking to her."

"Well," Vinny says, "maybe you're overestimating your natural charm."

Wayne ignores him. "It's this uniform. You put it on and you become like one of those guys—you know, with their balls chopped off?"

"Eunuchs," Vinny tells him.

"Yeah. Eunuchs, like in a harem. The uniform castrates you. Girls don't see past the polyester."

A guy in a slightly different uniform—I guess he's of higher rank—passes by our booth. "We need a mop-up in the back corner," he tells Wayne. "By the men's room."

"Got it," Wayne says, and makes like he's getting up until the other guy moves out of sight. "The assistant manager," he tells us. "He's about two years older than me. Clawed his way up. Now he thinks he's lord of the fries."

He sags back down in the seat beside me.

"Are you disobeying a direct order?" I say.

A shrug. "Minimum wage, minimum effort."

"That's pretty good. You think that up yourself?" Vinny says.

Wayne shakes his head, too depressed to rise to the bait. "It's written above the urinal in the staff washroom. I do all my reading there."

But eventually he does slouch off. "Minimum wage, maximum rage" is the last thing I hear as he goes off in search of a mop.

"Think we should bring him in on this?" Vin asks, salting his fries one at a time.

"Nah. You can't even take him to the library." I feel guilty saying it, seeing how Wayne's kind of my best friend. But he's got that habit of screwing things up. "Let's see the map again."

He opens it to Wilson Heights, and the red and green clusters. "This is his comfort zone," Vinny says. "Where he feels safe to do his thing. Somewhere in these six or seven blocks is our guy."

"Some of this stuff happened, what, ten years ago? What's to say he hasn't moved out of Grandma's house?"

"From reading the diary, I can't see him moving out. He's always talking about how he hates her, but how she has this power over him, like she's some kind of witch."

"So let's see," I say, trying to pull it together. "What do

we have? There's his target list of potential victims. We've narrowed down where he lives to a few blocks. What else do we know?"

"Okay. He's white, and—"

"Hold on. How do we know that?"

"The books say about ninety-nine percent of these wackos are white."

"Yeah? What's up with whitey?"

"Who knows. Anyway, using the dates of the clippings, and that one time early in the diary where he mentions how old he is, we can narrow his age down to early twenties."

I lean back, staring at the map and trying to make something out of all those dots, something like an X marking the spot. "We're looking for a white guy, early twenties, living with his grandmother in Wilson Heights." I drop the map on the table, shaking my head. "So basically, we still got squat."

Vinny shrugs. "We've got more than we had a couple of days ago."

"Yeah, but we're not closing the distance."

Growing up in the Jungle, you get programmed for failure. Most of the people who live there have the doomed look of lifers. They move in slow motion, never picking up enough speed to escape its gravity.

So deep down, I just expect to fail.

It's like I've skipped to the end of the textbook and looked at all the answers. I've seen the future. And I know I'm no hero. Last summer and the dead girl were just the

latest proof hammered into my head. So why I keep trying, I don't know.

I run my fingers over those colored dots, trying to read them like braille.

And I keep hearing something the coach of my old swim team used to say: "Doesn't matter who starts out in front. Matters who can close the distance."

TWENTY-THREE

I've gone through this book a dozen times now, searching for that place, the moment where he slips up and gives himself away. But Roach's paranoia kept him from saying anything that would betray his identity, in case the diary fell into enemy hands, I guess.

So I can't figure out why I'm stuck on this one page, about two-thirds of the way through the diary. I've gone over it before. There's nothing there. It's just another entry, cataloguing the details of one of his targets.

Bones, the anorexically thin woman with the pale skin and the sad face. Roach describes what she likes to read (thick romance novels), what she wears (baggy pastel clothes that hang on her), and the exact times of her arrival and departure at the subway. I can see him rushing home after stalking her to write this all down and relive it in his diary.

At the bottom of the page, he's written down a scrap of conversation he overheard between Bones and a friend. It's scribbled on a slip of paper, glued to the page. I can just see him fumbling through his pockets for something to jot their words down on before he forgot them. He refers to the friend as Skank.

Skank: Love that lipstick you're wearing. Is it Mac?
Bones: No. Revlon. Burgundy Flush. But it's too rich for my tone.
S: God. You've got such perfect skin. Like porcelain.
B: You're crazy. I'd kill for your tan. I'm like a ghost.
S: You shouldn't put yourself down so much.

That's all there is. Then Roach runs out of room on the scrap. It's a meaningless bit of conversation, doesn't go anywhere. So why am I stuck here, staring at it?

After another minute going in circles inside my head, I notice something about the paper. It's a plain, thin white slip, but it's got jagged edges on the ends, like it was torn off from a roll of paper. Like a receipt.

I stand and hold the paper up to the light. Beneath the scribbled conversation I can just make out something printed in ink on the other side. Using my thumbnail, I try and peel the slip off the page, but I have to stop when it starts to tear.

Ripping the page from the book, I go to the bathroom and turn the shower on, full-blast hot water. I wait as steam fills the room, wiping the sweat from my forehead. It takes a while, but as the steam builds into a fog the page gradually starts to warp. I grab Mom's tweezers and very, very slowly peel the slip off the page. I lose a couple of bits that refuse to pull away, but it's pretty much intact when it finally comes loose.

It's a receipt from Nut Factory Hardware Store. Under the name it says YORKDALE MALL. The purchases listed are for a padlock, eight stainless-steel screws, and sandpaper. A total of $22.69. It's dated last October. At the bottom of the receipt it says WE'RE NUTS ABOUT NUTS.

He shopped at Yorkdale last year. But so did a million other people. This is absolutely useless.

I let out a long sigh. The shower's still going and the steam is drenching me. I'm about to reach over and turn the water off when I notice something funny about how the prices are totaled up.

Blinking the sweat out of my eyes, I finally see the thing I've been searching for. The place where he gives himself away.

"What am I looking at?" Vin asks.

We're in the living room of his apartment, with its tangerine walls, burgundy couch, and amber carpeting. It looks like a sunset puked in here. It's closing in on nine in the morning and his mom has already left for work, so we've got the place to ourselves.

"It's a receipt," I tell him.

"I can see that. Why am I supposed to care?"

"I peeled it off a page in his diary."

"Right. So he shopped at Yorkdale a year ago. Not exactly a hot lead."

I'm sort of pleased that I'm ahead of Vin for once, pointing out what he's not seeing.

"Look at the line between the subtotal and the taxes."

He holds the slip up to inspect it.

"Ten percent off," he says. "So they had a sale?"

I shake my head. "Look at the letters beside the ten percent."

"Emp dis," Vin reads. "What is that, Latin?"

I allow myself a small smile. "Emp dis: employee discount."

He locks eyes with me, then studies the receipt under the lamp. "No way."

"Yeah."

"He works at a hardware store?"

I shrug. "Guess he's got to work somewhere."

Vin walks over to the windows, thinking it all through. He peels back a section of the tinfoil that covers the glass to block out the harsh sun in the afternoon. White morning light shines on the street outside.

"Where do we go from here?" he says.

TWENTY-FOUR

Dad would love this place. It's a tool guy's dream. There's a whole long aisle devoted to screws and nuts. They have screwdrivers ranging from mouse-sized to ones they must use on aircraft carriers. Every tool known to man.

I wander down the aisles of the Nut Factory, getting the feel of the place. Vinny's watching from out in the mall.

I've spotted two guys working right now, helping people find stuff. Besides them there's the cashier, a woman. I walk over to her.

"Hi. I was wondering if you're hiring right now?"

She shakes her head. "Not at the moment."

"Ah," I say, trying to look disappointed. "I hear you get a ten-percent discount working here."

"No. Twenty-five, actually," she tells me.

"Twenty-five?"

"Yep. Ten percent is what the mall staff gets."

"You mean, like people working in the other stores?"

She shakes her head. "No. Like the maintenance workers, administration, security guards."

"Really?" I say. "Okay, thanks."

Walking out of the store, I go over to where Vinny's sucking down an iced coffee. This whole thing just got way more complicated.

"So?" he says.

"He doesn't work there."

"No?"

I explain the ten-percent discount. "And there's got to be a hundred people cleaning and guarding and administrating this place. No way we can go through them all."

"Wait up," Vin says. "Maybe we can narrow it down."

"How?"

"Let me think a sec." He chews on his straw. "Sometimes these guys find it hard keeping a job. They've got, like, antisocial behavior and they hate authority, so that gets in the way. When they do manage to hang on to a job it's low-level, unskilled."

"So—what, you're thinking janitor or something?"

He shrugs. "Could be. But then there's also the type that goes for a job where they have control over other people. I was reading how a lot of serial killers try to get on the police force at some point, but they always fail the psych test. So they get a job that's *like* being a cop—private investigator, something military, or . . ." He leaves it for me to finish.

"Security guard."

"It fits," Vinny says. "The job would give him, like, the illusion of power. I can't see this guy in administration, or anywhere you'd need social skills."

"But he could be one of the maintenance workers, scrubbing toilets, mopping up."

Vinny makes a face, shaking his head. "Possibly. But it doesn't feel right."

"No. It doesn't."

I make up my mind, squashing all my doubts. Nobody's ever accused me of thinking things all the way through before I act. Look before you leap, people have been telling me for the last seventeen years. But that's just not me.

"He's a guard," I say. "Got to be."

Jacob sounded pissed when I called in sick today. You don't get sick days, he said. Food poisoning, I told him.

I'd go crazy sitting around in the dungeon all day when I've got Roach in my sights now.

It takes a while to find the Yorkdale security office. It's tucked out of the way, down a hall past a long row of pay phones and doors marked MAINTENANCE and ELECTRICAL. I push through the door into a reception area.

An Asian guy with slicked-back hair sits at a desk, talking on the phone. He's wearing a gray and blue uniform with SECURITY printed above the breast pocket. Behind him, there's another door leading to a back room with rows of security monitors, showing a couple dozen views of the mall.

Waiting for him to get off the phone, I look around the room. On a bulletin board, under the heading YORKDALE'S TEN LEAST WANTED is a group of Polaroids showing notorious shoplifters. Beside them there's a poster showing three multiracial guards with the caption WE'RE WATCHING TO KEEP YOU SAFE.

"Can I help you?" the guy at the desk asks, hanging up the phone.

Because he's Asian, I've already crossed him off the list in my head. Doesn't fit the profile—not white. But how solid is that profile we put together, anyway? I mean, we might as well have pulled it out of a cereal box for all the expertise me and Vin have between us.

"Hi. I was thinking of applying for security work at the mall."

"We're not hiring right now," he tells me. "But you're welcome to fill out an application. We keep them on file for six months." He pauses, listening to a staticky voice on the walkie-talkie strapped to his shoulder. Then he presses a button and says, "Copy."

I nod. "Sure. I'll take an application. That would be great."

In the monitor room the lights are slightly dimmed, making the screens glow a green-tinged black and white. I can hear a couple of voices talking baseball in there.

He grabs the form from a filing cabinet.

"Here you go," he says.

"So how many guards work here?" I ask casually.

"About fifteen. More around Christmas."

"I guess you have to work different shifts."

He nods. "Three shifts: six A.M. to two; two to ten; ten to six. Round the clock."

"Okay, thanks. I'll fill this out and get it back to you."

I leave the office and walk down the hall, staring at the floor, trying to fit all the information together. Someone passing by bumps my arm.

"Sorry," I say absently, looking over in time to see the gray and blue security uniform going past. I turn to watch the guard push through into the office. He's red-haired and skinny, a little taller than me.

He disappears, and I stand there wondering—Is it you? Are you the one? Somehow I think I'll know Roach when I see him—I've spent so much time inside his head. But even in my dreams all I see of him is his shadow.

Vinny's waiting in front of a pet store, watching brightly colored fish swim circles in their aquariums.

I hand him the application. "Here. Get a job, you bum."

He vacuums up the last of his iced coffee with his straw. "Do they get to carry those Taser guns, the ones that zap you with a thousand volts?" I shake my head. "No? How about batons?" Another shake. "Pepper spray? Anything?"

"Just a polyester uniform, a bad haircut, and a walkie-talkie."

"I'll stick to being a bum. Better hours."

We could break up and cover more ground in the mall, but I think we'll do better with two sets of eyes focusing on the same thing. That way me and Vin can debate who looks like the most promising candidate.

Picking up a box of doughnut holes and an Orange Julius, we grab a seat by the escalator on level two. A high-traffic area, with a clear view of the hallway that leads to the security office.

"So what've we got?" I say. "Fifteen guards, working on three shifts?"

Vinny examines a doughnut hole before popping it into his mouth. "On the graveyard shift they'd only have a skeleton crew working," he adds, licking the glaze off his fingers. "Say, three of them."

"Okay, so that leaves us with six working the morning shift and six for the afternoon, roughly." I notice Vin digging around trying to pick out the best holes. "Hey, don't be taking all the chocolate ones."

"Come on, I'm not exactly getting paid for this, you know."

"What about that Orange Julius you're drinking, and—" I stop, seeing the red-haired guard who passed by me in the hall. "What about this guy?"

We watch him walk briskly away.

"Put him on the list," Vin says. "We'll call him Red."

He gets up and leans on the railing, sipping his drink and looking down at the crowds on level one. "Okay, I've got a theory. Remember the women on his hit list, how he had their schedules, their subway stops, and all that? Well, the times he had listed were all between ten-thirty and eleven-thirty. And the stops were all within fifteen minutes of here."

I sit there in silence, trying to figure out his point. "And . . . ?"

"Try this out," Vin says. "He gets off work at ten and rides the trains, hunting. That would explain the time frame and the locations of the stops he's staked out."

"So he works the closing shift."

"Makes sense," he says. "He does the two-to-ten shift, then squeezes in some stalking before heading home to Granny."

"Hey," I say, shifting things around in my head. "You know that time I followed the woman from his hit list, the one he calls Cherry? She got on the subway at Yorkdale Station. I remember thinking how she looked like she'd just got off work. She was wearing a skirt and tights, but she had running shoes on, like she'd finished work and didn't want to wear her heels home."

"Then she works at the mall?"

"Maybe. Yeah. When I saw her, it was after ten. Closing time."

"What stop did she get off at?" Vinny asks. "Where does she live?"

"Near Wilson Station." It takes me a moment, but then things stop shifting and fall into place. "Not far from where all those dots on your map connect. Right in his comfort zone."

I take a deep breath and blow it out. I lean back, looking way up to the big skylight. Dark clouds have rolled in, blocking the sun, promising the first rain in forever.

"If he's working till closing, he should be here right now," I say. "Starting his shift."

"Yeah, but that's a whole lot of guessing going on there," Vin mumbles, tossing back another doughnut hole.

Glancing down, I catch sight of a large woman with short blond hair wearing security's gray and blue uniform.

"Hey, check this out," I say.

"That makes three now, including the guy you talked to in the office. Three down, three to go."

After an hour, my butt hasn't just fallen asleep, it's gone into a coma. Vinny's powered through a second box of doughnut holes and paces around and around like a mosquito. We've counted five guards.

The Asian guy and the woman don't fit the profile—not white, not male. Same goes for a black guard Vin spotted. We catch sight of an older guard dragging a very reluctant kid down the hall to the office. Too old to be a contender.

Then there's Red. He's got potential.

I get up and try to stretch some feeling back into my numb butt. Vinny's been ranting for the past ten minutes about how *Terminator 3* didn't measure up to the first two, and I'm about ready to toss him over the railing.

"Wait up. Here we go," he says.

"Where?"

Vin points down to level one. "Number six. Our final contestant."

The guard walking past the Body Shop is a big guy. Maybe two hundred and sixty pounds, six feet, and stretching the polyester uniform like Schwarzenegger in spandex. He looks to be in his mid-twenties, has wavy black hair, dark eyes, mustache. He passes beneath us, out of sight.

I keep expecting something, a jolt of recognition. All I get is confusion, trying to see evil in these strangers' faces. The thing they say about serial killers—they look pretty normal, nothing special. They look like you and me. What sets them apart is invisible, their lack of conscience, their need to control and manipulate, and kill.

"What do we do now?" Vinny asks.

I look down at the crowds of afternoon shoppers, trying to clear my head, to see the next move. Now that we've finally started to close the distance, I'm kind of in shock. This might actually work.

"Now we take the next step," I hear myself saying. "We follow them home."

TWENTY-FIVE

It's after five when I get back to the Jungle. I left Vinny at the 7-Eleven; he had to pick up some stuff for his mom. The plan is to meet up later, waiting till about nine to head out.

In front of B building, on a lawn that's more dirt than grass, Wayne's lying on a towel, tanning. An empty Big Gulp cup and a Chee-tos bag are discarded beside him. He's all oiled and shiny in the late sun. I notice his head is shaved again, smooth as a cue ball and almost as white.

"Hey, man," I say. "Shouldn't you be flipping burgers right about now?"

Wayne lifts his sunglasses to squint at me. "No way. I'm a free man."

"Free how?"

"Free, as in they fired my butt," he says. "Retired my uniform."

"For what, bad hygiene?"

He leans up on his elbows, raising his glasses to rest on top of his bald head. "Last week, down at the Barn, six hundred bucks went missing in action."

"Six hundred? How?" I shake my head, trying to read Wayne's eyes for the answer I suspect. But he's reading mine, too.

"Don't look at me like that," he says.

"Well, did you?"

"If I was going to take six hundred—the way I'd do it, they'd never even know they had the money in the first place. This was done without finesse. Too obvious."

"Then why did you get canned?"

He sighs. "Guess I'm the usual suspect. Got that shifty look. And . . . I might have mentioned to one of the cashier girls about my past brushes with the law. I guess she passed it around."

Just like Wayne to try and score some bad boy points with a girl, bragging about his life of crime.

"Even when I'm clean they think I'm dirty," he tells me. "I mean, maybe I skimmed a twenty now and then, but they never even knew about that."

"So you were taking a commission?"

"Min-i-mum wage, man! When they pay you squat they expect a little—what's the word—pilferage. Besides, that's not the point. The point is I got shafted. Unjustly accused."

Back when we got busted in the great toilet heist, my life of crime ended, but Wayne's only paused long enough for the heat to die down. He always has some scam he's working on. It's like a hobby to him. Years ago, he tried to teach me how to pick a lock, but I just didn't have the touch for it.

He could do it in his sleep. Wayne's a natural, but his criminal ambitions only go as far as what he likes to call victimless crimes. He's like those vegetarians who won't eat anything that ever had a face—Wayne won't do a crime with a face on it.

"You told me you were going straight," I say.

"I am. As of right now. Consider what I just told you my confession." He smiles. "So, do you absolve me of my sins?"

Wayne's always going to be Wayne, and his half-assed attempts at staying legal are part of his charm, I guess. But there's a sadness in his smile, and a kind of worn-out edge to his words. Like even *he's* grown tired of the part he's playing.

"My son," I tell him, shaking my head. "You're absolved."

He lies back on the towel. "My soul feels clean again."

If only it was that easy.

"Later," I say, leaving Wayne to crisp in the sun.

When I walk in the door, Mom says there's a voice-mail message for me.

"Who from?"

"Kim," she says, with a raised eyebrow.

In the living room, I pick up the phone and play the message.

"Hey, Duncan. It's me, Kim. According to the display on my phone, you've called four times in the last week. And left zero messages. What's up?"

Did I really call that much? After the first time, I phoned

when I knew she wouldn't be home, just to hear her voice on the message. Kind of pathetic, but I got my little fix that way.

"If you need to talk," she goes on, "you know, we can still talk to each other. We're not mortal enemies. Anyway, I'm late for practice. I've got a game tomorrow night down in Amesbury Park. So this is me leaving a message. See, it's not so hard. It won't hurt. See ya."

Then comes the beep, and a computer voice asking if I want to save this message. I press three to save.

She's playing down in the park tomorrow. Maybe I could go. We can still talk. It's not so hard, Kim says. But it is. Some people you can't be friends with, not when you've been something more.

I crash on the couch and turn on the TV.

Dad comes out of his vampire hibernation a while later, looking like the undead. His hair is plastered flat on one side of his head and sticking straight up on the other. The blackout mask he uses to pretend it's night hangs under his chin. On the way to the bathroom, he squints at me like I look familiar but he can't exactly place me.

"Morning, Dad," I say.

"Huh?" he grunts, then remembers to take out his earplugs.

"I said good morning."

"Right. Hi, kid."

Dad tries to put the earplugs in his pocket, but seeing

how he's only wearing boxers, there aren't any. He keeps trying, though, as he stumbles off toward the bathroom.

A minute later I hear the water go on. He lets out a yelp. Ever since the heat wave crashed down on us, Dad's been taking his showers cold. He calls it his arctic defibrillator because it shocks his heart back to life. I can hear him gasping.

In the kitchen Mom's making pizza—well, not actually making, more like defrosting. When it comes out of the box it looks like a cheese-plastered manhole cover, which is close to how it tastes. Because it's not real cheese, nothing that's seen the inside of a cow. It's soy cheese. No cholesterol, no heart attacks, no flavor.

On TV, *Entertainment Tonight* is starting. Mary Hart has her serious face on. A minor celebrity has died. They have reactions from other celebrities. He died so young, it's so tragic. When the story ends, Mary perks up instantly to tell us about the new Pepsi commercial. It's all pleasantly shallow. Nothing to worry about, nothing to keep you up nights. I wish I could just sink into the couch and zone out for a couple of weeks.

But there's a little leather book, with a cover that feels like skin, hiding in my closet.

When me and Dad used to go fishing, years ago, we would catch fish and just throw them back. We were only there for the hell of it, and it didn't seem to hurt the fish much past a cut lip. But then we'd get one that would swallow the hook. We knew he was a goner, whether we tried to pull it out or just cut the line. Because once you've swallowed the hook, there's no losing it. Me, I've swallowed it big-time.

Dad walks out of the bathroom in his robe, combing his wet hair. "I'm back from the dead," he announces.

"Right in time for breakfast," says Mom, coming in for a quick kiss.

"You taste like cheese," he tells her.

"I'm making you an egg-white omelet. The rest of us are having pizza."

"For breakfast?"

She rubs her fingers over his stubbly cheek. "It's only breakfast on your side of the world."

Dad sits down on his recliner. He bends his comb and flicks a few drops of water at me on the couch. "How you handling it, kid?"

I give him a blank look. My brain's running in circles, going over my plan for tonight, so he catches me off guard.

"The job," he says. "How you handling it?"

"Oh. You know, it's pretty much a mind-numbing, soul-killing waste of time."

Dad nods, easing back in his chair and putting his feet up. "Wiser words were never said. That's why you have to go to college, get a future. They used to have this program for rotten kids, where they'd take them into prisons to meet the real hard-core bad guys—to scare them straight. Think of your job that way. You don't want to end up with a life sentence."

"If this job was supposed to be a lesson, then I think I've learned it already. Can I quit now?"

He throws his comb at me. "Flick around and see if there's a Blue Jays game on."

When breakfast/dinner is ready, Dad drags in one of the big box fans from their bedroom and positions it so we all get our slice of the breeze. We sit and eat and watch baseball, which must be the most boring sport ever invented. But right here and now, I love it. I love this boring, ordinary meal. Freeze the frame here, and let it last.

It's like the eye of the storm. Everything's calm and quiet, and I can almost forget what's supposed to happen tonight. So long as I don't look up and see the wall of the storm that's spinning around me, waiting for my next move.

TWENTY-SIX

We're set up at the entrance to the Yorkdale subway station, waiting for the mall to close and our prime suspects to appear.

"You take the cell," Vinny says. He borrowed his mother's cell phone for tonight, so we can hook up after we're done tailing these guys home. Whoever has the phone will have to wait for the other to call.

"Why me?"

"Because, I saw on *Sixty Minutes* how this brand gives off the highest radiation. Thing should come with a Geiger counter. My mother got it years ago. It's prehistoric."

"No one ever got cancer from using a cell phone." I give him a look.

"Not yet. But give it a few years."

"Besides, you should keep it. Then I can call you from a pay phone and keep track of you."

Vin shakes his head. "No way. I don't even stay in the room when the microwave's on."

Bringing the cell was a good idea. I should have thought of it and taken one from work.

According to our synchronized watches, it's now 10:05. We've narrowed down our hit list to two: the guard we're calling Red, and the guy we're calling Jumbo, the steroid case with the mustache.

Mom's soy-cheese pizza is dying a slow death in my gut, making me crabby. It's bugging me that Vin won't take the phone. If something happens to him, it's on me. I dragged him here.

"Last night I rented *The Silence of the Lambs*," Vin tells me. "And *American Psycho*. Tried to pick up some tips."

"Those aren't exactly FBI training films. The pros say all those movies are ridiculous, anyway. They make the killers into these comic-book supervillains, when most of the time it's just the quiet guy next door."

Vinny's wearing his usual—army surplus jacket, jeans, ratty sneakers. I'm all in black, T-shirt and jeans and base-ball cap, wearing my steel-toed army boots just in case. Vin brought his Swiss Army knife—the idiot thing weighs about two pounds and includes scissors and a corkscrew. So he can crack open some wine after he gives the nut a haircut.

"Don't take any chances," I tell him. "No approaching him or saying anything to him. If he sees you, or gets suspicious at all, then just bail, okay?"

"Yes, Mom."

"Keep your distance. All we want is an address. Even if you lose him before he gets home, we'll know if he lives in the right area, the right neighborhood."

"What is this, Stalking 101?"

"And take the stupid phone," I tell him.

"No way."

I give up, and make sure he at least has change for a pay phone. Vinny keeps joking around, but I can see he's nervous. And excited. He's seen too many movies.

The last shoppers, kicked out at closing time, pass by us. Then I catch sight of the old guard as he goes through the turnstiles and up the escalator to the platform.

When 10:15 rolls around, Vin says, "So we have to decide who gets who."

"Right." Who gets who? "I'll take whoever comes first. If you think about it, one of them might not even show. He might have a car. But Roach, he'll definitely take the subway. It's like his own twisted buffet table."

Vinny kicks my foot. I look at him, then follow his eyes to the guy approaching the entrance.

Jumbo. Out of uniform, wearing an extra-extra-large Raptors windbreaker over a white T-shirt. I guess I'm up. Before I go, I turn to Vin.

"No risks," I say.

He pats the bulge in his pocket. His Swiss Army knife. "Don't worry. I'm packing a corkscrew."

I try a smile, but it dies on my face. Giving Jumbo a head start, I wait until he's halfway up the escalator before I hop on. This guy's got muscles I never even knew existed. He could squash me like a bug.

I'll just take the advice I gave Vin—lay low, keep some distance, don't push it.

Yorkdale has an elevated outdoor subway station, open to the night air. I turn my back to Jumbo when I see which side of the platform he's waiting on, making like I'm looking off down the tracks for the next train. The sky is gray with city lights bouncing off the clouds. I swipe a drop of sweat from my eyebrow. A couple minutes tick by; then I see Red come off the escalator.

Caught between two suspects, I shift my gaze to the bubble gum poster on the other side of the tracks. For a second it looks like Red might be going the same way as Jumbo, which would be great—I could keep track of Vinny. But then he moves off behind me to the other side of the platform.

Seconds later, Vin shows up. He glances in my direction, then past me to where Red's waiting, and I'm worried he's going to wink or nod or something stupid. But he moves on like a stranger.

Their train comes first. I watch as Vinny gets on the same car as Red.

Damn. It's the first car—Roach always rides up front. Where me and Jumbo are standing on this side of the platform, we'll be boarding in the middle of the train. Vinny's back is to me when he takes a seat inside. I have to stop myself from racing over to join him. Too late now, anyway. His train pulls out as mine rushes in.

I get on and keep an eye on the big guy, watching his reflection in the night-mirrored glass as the train races along beside the 401 highway. Jumbo stares off into space, not even noticing the two women on the train. I glance at him sideways, trying to catch him doing something suspicious. Something to give him away. But he has the same bored look as every other passenger. I'm not getting any weird vibes off him.

We ride to the end of the line. At Downsview Station, he gets off and I wait until the doors start to close to follow, giving the big guy some room. Jumbo walks to the end of the platform and takes the stairs to the surface.

This exit leads onto a side street. As I reach the top of the stairs, I see that he's stopped about ten feet away. I freeze, not sure what my next move should be.

He catches sight of something and hurries off down the sidewalk. I give him a good thirty feet, matching his pace. The streetlights are widely spaced in this neighborhood, leaving pools of darkness between them. Another block and he'll reach the main street.

Ahead of him, I see the smaller figure of a woman passing from the light into shadow. She's small and thin, wearing shorts and a T-shirt. Jumbo speeds up, closing in on her.

My vision tunnels in on the two converging shadows. He's going to grab her before she can make it to the safety of the lights ahead on the main street. My heart stutters in shock, and I break into a jog. I'm still twenty feet back when Jumbo reaches her. He grabs her from behind and lifts her in the air like she weighs nothing. I hear her let out a breathless yelp. And with a little, effortless toss he spins her in the air and catches her, so she's facing him.

I stumble and almost fall on my face, but manage to regain my footing, looking up in time to see them kiss. I stop dead in my tracks, standing there in the shadows.

"You idiot!" she says, laughing and shouting at the same time. "Where did you come from?"

He sets her down. "Took the side exit."

"Give me a heart attack! You're buying me dinner now."

They start walking again toward the main street. I watch them go, breathing hard, blinking the sweat from my eyes.

One thing I know from the books is that most serial killers don't have close relationships with women.

I look up as the clouded night sky rumbles with thunder.

Now it all depends on Vinny. The odds that Red is the one just shot up.

Why couldn't he just take the stupid phone?

Where do I go now? All I can do is wait for Vin to call. Taking the phone out of my pocket, I make sure it's on and then just stare at it for a minute, commanding it to ring. But I only left him fifteen minutes ago.

In the summer, Toronto doesn't go to sleep till the early morning hours, and even then it's a restless sleep for the air-conditioning deprived. Leaning against a newspaper box, I watch the crowd. People rush down the stairs to catch their trains, and others drag themselves up from the depths. Laughter comes from the patio of an Italian restaurant across the street.

I think back to the night I followed Cherry home, walking in his footsteps. Watching the women go by, I try to see them the way *he* does: as cold, alien creatures, rejecting and humiliating. But all I see are victims-to-be, walking on the edge.

Going back underground, I check my watch. It's been twenty-five minutes since we parted ways. I have to start doing something before I lose it. Vinny's train took him southbound, so at least if I take the train down a few stops I'll be closer to wherever he is now. I hope.

Going past Yorkdale, Lawrence West, and Glencairn Stations, I stand by the doors, keeping an eye out for Vin's green army jacket. This part of the subway line runs above ground, so any second now Vin could call, telling me he's safe. And we could have a laugh. After Eglinton West there's a long ten-minute stretch between stops, and I stare past my reflection in the glass at the streetlights whipping by.

Thirty-seven minutes. Vin should have called by now if he was following another dead end. Back at Yorkdale, he was cracking jokes like we're playing some kind of game. I brought him into this. Anything happens to him, it's on me.

The wheels of the train let out a high-pitched squeal as we take a turn. I lean against the door, feeling cold sweat run down my back.

Forty-five minutes, and still between stops.

Too long! This is way too long. There are phones everywhere. There's no reason to take this amount of time, unless Vinny's found something and tracked Red home. Or maybe he can't call. Maybe someone's stopping him.

Get a grip! Shut up, don't think like that.

Finally, the train pulls into St. Clair West and I scan the people on the elevated platform for a familiar face. Should I get off here? How far do I go?

The train slows to a halt, and I nearly jump out of my skin when the phone in my hand rings. I almost drop the stupid thing, trying to press the button to answer.

"Yes?" I shout into it, covering my other ear against the noise of the doors opening and an announcement over the station P.A.

"What?" comes a voice on the other end, the static making it unidentifiable.

"Who is this?" I say.

"It's me."

As I step out onto the platform, the P.A. shuts up.

"Thank hell," I say.

"Speak up, man. Can't hear you through the radiation."

"Where are you?"

"About three blocks from Spadina Station."

"What happened?"

"Followed Red home."

"He lives by Spadina?" I have to raise my voice to make sure I'm getting through. This thing's a piece of crap.

"Yeah. I tailed him to a Seven-Eleven, then to his house.

I walked by the place a couple times. Guy's got a wife and kid. And a Chihuahua. I really don't think he's the one."

I slouch over, squeezing my eyes shut. None of that sounds right for our guy. We're looking for a loner, and if he has a dog it'll be something vicious, a rottweiler or a pit bull. Not a little midget dog.

"You get anything?" Vin asks.

"Nah. Struck out."

"So where does that leave us?" he says. Not really a question because he knows the answer.

I watch the rear lights of the train I was on shrinking in the darkness of the tunnel until they're swallowed up.

"Leaves us nowhere," I say.

TWENTY-SEVEN

Busy morning in the dungeon. As punishment for calling in sick yesterday, Jacob's making me load the unclaimed junk for the YMCA sale into their truck. The driver said he's got a bad back. "I'm paid to drive. The only thing I lift is my own fat butt." So I put the boxes on a dolly, take the elevator up to the surface.

The drought broke last night, somewhere around three A.M. I must have finally drifted off, lying in bed with all the sheets pushed onto the floor. A wicked thunderstorm woke me up, the rain falling so hard it sounded like hail ricocheting off the windows. Getting up to close my window, I got sprayed by a gust of cool rain. Felt so good I stood there a minute getting wet, shivering when the thunder cracked close by.

Storm clouds are still darkening the sky today, tinted with that faint yellow color they get around here when a thunderstorm's brewing. The air feels heavy and electric. I dodge puddles in the alley, wheeling the dolly up to the truck. The driver's having a smoke, supervising.

Last night's dead ends really knocked the wind out of me and Vinny. We hardly spoke after we met up again for the ride back to the Jungle. What's to say? The whole thing was a washout. What a mess. All our theories and strategies added up to a big fat waste of time. The pressure I've been feeling, knowing the clock is running down, has eaten out a cold hollow space in my gut. But something changed last night. Something clicked inside me, or cracked inside me, and I suddenly got this feeling—that somewhere in the city, the clock has already run out, and the explosion was just too far away for me to hear.

Too late and too far away.

After dumping my load of boxes I go back down to make another run.

I'm surprised by how many there are to haul up, even though I packed them all. I'm even more surprised that pitching all this junk doesn't begin to make a dent down in the dungeon. The shelves are still jammed. Dust bunnies run wild down the aisles, waiting for me to sweep them back under the stacks.

Up and down I go, like a minimum-wage yo-yo. When the last box is heaved into the truck, the driver looks at the cardboard mess in back and says, "Nice job."

He disappears around the side of the truck, so he doesn't hear the "Up yours" I send his way.

Back underground, I grab a drink from the water cooler. Jacob's listening to the radio. All news. All boring. Until one story stops me dead.

"Police and transit authorities are investigating an accident involving a forty-year-old woman hit by a subway train at Queen Station early last night. Witnesses reported that the woman was pushed into the path of an oncoming train, which was unable to brake in time. There are no suspects yet in custody, but police have a description. They are looking for a Hispanic male with a slim build and shoulder-length black hair, twenty-five to thirty-five years old. Transit authorities have handed over videotapes from the surveillance cameras at Queen Station. The victim was taken to Toronto General with severe head injuries. She is now on a respirator in what the doctors describe as a profound coma. Due to extensive brain damage, it is not known when or if she will awaken. Her name is being withheld pending notification of next of kin. . . . A seven-week-long drought ended last night, and more thunderstorms are forecast for today. . . ."

Leaning against the wall by the cooler, with an empty paper cup in my hand, I stare at the radio sitting on the counter. A woman pushed. In the subway. Five minutes from here.

The air suddenly feels too thick to breathe. Good thing I'm leaning on something or my legs might give out on me. I hear myself thinking: *He did it. Did it. Did it.* The words run through my head like a stutter. My brain's frozen in a loop.

The sound on the radio snaps off, and I look over to see Jacob sitting hunched over the counter, his head bowed, eyes closed. I can hear him breathing heavily. It takes me a second to untangle his reaction from mine.

Then I remember his wife, and what the transit cop said about a stroke and her turning into a vegetable. Dying in slow motion.

We're trapped down here together, refugees from the real world. We can't save anybody. A girl, a wife, an innocent woman on the subway.

After a minute, breathing is still an effort for me, but my legs feel steadier. I drop my cup in the garbage. Jacob glances over, irritated, like I just woke him up. He looks a thousand years old and ready to drop.

"Why don't you go find something to do," he tells me, his voice scratchy. Translation: *Get lost.*

Back in the stacks I grab my lawn chair and collapse on it. After ten minutes staring at the wall the first shock fades enough for me to think again.

A pusher? Doesn't seem right for Roach. It's too . . . I don't know, too clean somehow. Shoving someone off a subway platform wouldn't give Roach the kind of thrill he's looking for.

"Kid." Jacob's voice startles me. He's standing at the end of the row. I've never seen him in the stacks. "I'm on lunch," he says, and walks off.

It's just past eleven o'clock, and he never goes till twelve. He's religious about lunchtime. I tried to switch lunch hours with him one time to grab a bite with Vinny, but he shot me down. I give him a minute to clear out, then take his seat at the counter and turn the radio back on. At the half hour the news repeats, but there's nothing new on the woman in a coma.

A couple of fourteen-year-old girls come in looking for sunglasses. They're what Jacob calls shoppers, people who come in trying to claim stuff they never lost. Rainy days they ask for umbrellas—but they don't know when they lost them or what exactly they look like. These days they try to scam sunglasses, but they're never sure what color the frames were, the make, or when they lost them. If they're too vague, your lie detector goes off.

Sorry, I tell them. I can't help you.

I scan Jacob's newspaper for anything suspicious—disappearances, attacks—but I don't see Roach's hand anywhere. An Italian guy comes asking about a wrench set he forgot on the bus on his way home from work. And, a miracle, I actually find it. He's so thrilled he wants to give me a tip. I say, "No. No, I can't." But he presses a five into my hand and I don't press it back. I *did* make the guy's day.

At about twelve-thirty, Jacob's still not back. The phone rings.

"Transit. Lost and found," I say.

"Duncan."

"Oh, hey, Vinny. What's going on?"

"I'm watching TV."

"That's a wild life you got there."

"The noon news is on," he says.

"Oh." I know why he's calling now. Vin tells me what the news said, nothing more than I know already.

"So . . . ," he says.

"So?"

"We gotta give this up, man. We can turn over what we've got to the cops and let them run with it."

I say nothing.

"It's too dangerous," he goes on. "We followed our leads and came up with squat. I mean, this is someone's life we're playing with here."

Part of me wants to agree, to give in and give up what we know. But it feels wrong. I can't do it.

"Duncan, if he pushed that woman this morning—"

"It wasn't him." I break in on Vinny. "They say the pusher was Hispanic. We're looking for a white guy."

"Our guy could be a hunchbacked Indian dwarf for all we know."

"The whole thing—it's wrong for him. You saw the shots of what he did to those animals. That's how he gets his rush. He's a cutter, not a pusher."

"Says who? What do you know? You skim a couple books and suddenly you're some kind of FBI profiler. That's crap. You gotta let this go. What were you going to do even if you found the guy, flash your bus pass and put him under arrest?"

I let out a sigh. "I don't know."

"Exactly. You don't know. You're not thinking straight. The cops can track this guy down."

"The cops don't care. They don't have the time to hunt down potential killers—they've got real ones crawling all over them. We're getting close here, Vin."

"We're getting nowhere. What if the guy doesn't even work at the mall anymore? What if he's a janitor there, or some office geek in administration? You gonna follow everybody home?"

"I don't know." That's all I can think to say. But it pretty much says it all. I don't know anything anymore. Even the most concrete lead I've got, the receipt, could be nothing. What's to say he didn't just pick it up off the floor of the subway for something to scribble on? He could be anywhere. Anyone.

It's quiet on both ends of the line.

"Okay," I say. "Look, you don't have to be in on this anymore. It's my problem."

"It's not that easy, man," he says. "I can't just sit on this and wait till bodies start turning up."

"Give me some time."

"Might not be any time left."

We kick it around some more and agree to meet after I get off work. I know what he's saying, and maybe he's right. I'm out of my league. I can't save anyone.

But I just can't let it go.

TWENTY-EIGHT

When Jacob finally gets back around two, I can tell he's had a liquid lunch. And by liquid I don't mean a protein shake, not unless they've started making them with vodka. It isn't obvious or anything. But if you see someone eight hours a day, five days a week, you know what to expect from them. So when he starts talking to me more than his usual grouching and grunts, I know something's up.

"You know," he says, leaning back in his chair and staring at the ceiling. "Nothing ever changes down here. Could be summer up on the surface, could be winter. But the temperature in this room stays the same. The seasons can't reach this far down. You know what the drivers and the conductors call this place?"

I shrug. "The dungeon?" My own pet name for it.

"Hah. No. They call it the morgue. Where careers come to die."

My brain's already exhausted and I'm not in the mood to listen, but this is the only time he's ever really talked to me.

"This is where they put you on ice," he mumbles.

"So *they* sent you down here?"

He takes so long to answer I'm thinking he didn't hear me. But then he says: "No. I put myself on ice."

I could ask why, but I already know the story.

"I'm the only driver who ever asked to come down here." He tugs at his ear thoughtfully. "This is where they used to send suspended drivers. I thought I'd only stay a few weeks, but I found out I fit here in the morgue. It's quiet, nothing changes. The world could go up in smoke and we wouldn't feel a thing."

Jacob fixes on me with his booze-blurred eyes.

"But you don't belong here, kid," he says. "When your time's up, just run and don't look back."

He leans back in his chair and closes his eyes like he's going to doze off.

Jacob's wrong about me, though. I belong here as much as he does. We're both in hiding; he's just been at it longer.

"I'm going to go get some lunch," I say, not sure if he's still conscious.

His eyes stay closed, but he says, "Go ahead."

Back in the stacks, I grab the pair of sunglasses I skimmed out of one of the Y sale boxes. Their time has expired, and I know they'll look perfect on me. I hear the dungeon door open and close, and I'm wiping the glasses on my jeans to clean some dust when the bell rings.

What part of "I'm on lunch" does the old man not understand?

When I get to the front, there's a guy standing on the

other side of the counter. He's wearing glasses thick enough to distort his eyes, making them look larger than they should. Jacob glances back at me.

"Before you go," he says, "check for one more thing. Looking for a book."

"What's the title?" I ask.

Jacob shakes his head. "He says there's no title, just a plain cover. A brown leather-bound book, with yellow edges on the pages. Lost it a couple weeks ago. Check the shelves."

I stare back at Jacob. I think my heart stops beating—I'm definitely not breathing. I don't move my head, but my eyes shift to where the man with the glasses is standing. He's about six feet tall and looks solid, with dark buzz-cut hair. His face is seriously acne-scarred. He looks back at me like I'm an insect he's thinking of stepping on.

"Sometime today!" Jacob prods me.

That breaks me out of it. I manage to turn and disappear into the stacks.

I never dreamed he might come looking for his diary. Right now, the book is sitting in my closet under my old hockey equipment. And now, after all the time I've spent searching for him, Roach comes and finds me.

I know you, I want to shout at him. I know what you are.

I stare at the shelves in a blind confusion, swallowing back a growing panic. I breathe in deeply and let it out with a shudder.

Get a grip! Focus! What do I do, now that I've found him?

After another ragged breath, it comes to me. Simple. Follow him home, get an address, then hand everything over to the cops in a nice little package.

That's the plan, only like all my plans it's kind of blurry—I'm not big on thinking things through. That's what Vinny's for. But there's no time anyway. Just act normal. Like all roaches, he's probably super-sensitive to what's going on around him. I don't want to suddenly turn on the lights and lose him when he runs and hides.

I give it another half minute, like I'm actually looking for his book. Then I walk back to the counter with a blank face.

"No. Nothing," I tell him. "Must not have been turned in."

There's a weird moment there where Roach just stares at me with his strangely vacant mud-brown eyes. Distorted behind those lenses, they seem to see more than they should, and more deeply. Then he grunts, turns to the door and leaves.

Jacob eases back into his chair again, staring into space with his eyelids drooping.

I grab a clean-looking Budweiser cap off the top of the New Arrivals box. I make sure there's nothing disgusting inside and put it on. I've got my shades, too. Now that Roach has seen me, I'll need a little camouflage.

"Okay," I tell Jacob. "I'm taking off now."

But he's already dozing, chin drooping toward his chest.

I listen by the door until I hear the elevator closing in the hall; then I bolt. The elevator moves like an arthritic turtle. Taking the stairs two at a time, I can beat or at least tie him on a race to the subway level. Still, it's six flights of stairs, and my lungs give out around five. The stairwell feels as if it's been sucked dry of oxygen. I stumble and end up taking the last flight using my hands as well as my feet.

Opening the door at the top, I look down the wide hall, past the maintenance offices to where the elevator doors are closing. There he is, walking away. I notice for the first time he's wearing the blue shirt and gray pants that are part of the uniform of Yorkdale security. I give him some room, keeping pace, only rushing a bit when he gets to the end of the hall and turns left. I can't lose him now.

We go through the main entrance of Bay Station. There's enough of a crowd coming and going from downtown this afternoon that I can stay close but still hidden.

Following him down to the platform, I track where he looks and what he's looking at. Not real big on subtlety, Roach stares at the women he passes like he's at a strip club and they're here for his amusement. Maybe it's only because I know how he thinks, but the way he stares, he's not just undressing women with his eyes—he's dissecting them.

The train comes and Roach gets on the first car, like I knew he would. Now that he's told me his secrets, I know him better than anybody. Getting on the second car so he doesn't catch on to me, I stand watching through the window of the door that connects the cars.

We transfer at Spadina to another line, the one that leads out past Yorkdale, ending at Downsview. Everything's flowing now, and I can almost see his moves before he makes them. In my nightmares he was a faceless shadow, unreachable and unstoppable. Now that I have him in sight, he's shrunk down to human form, evil in a plain wrapper. And I've become the shadow, his shadow, following him all the way home.

I watch him watching potential targets. He must have been panicked when he realized his diary was missing, must have finally worked back in his head to where he lost it. All his twisted fantasies spelled out. I'm sure he never dreamed his precious book would be used to bring him down.

I'm expecting him to get off at Yorkdale—makes sense if he's working two to ten—but we pass it by and he's still here. I breathe out a sigh. If he'd gone to work, it would have meant more late-night surveillance, waiting till his shift ended. But now it looks like he's leading me straight back to his comfort zone. Me and Vinny focused on the closing shift at the mall, which made sense, considering Roach's target list and hunting times. But it's looking like he worked six A.M. to two, then came over to the lost and found. I guess even a killer has to work a different shift occasionally.

Getting off at Wilson Station, I trail him to the bus loop. This is the tricky part. I have to get on the bus with him. There's no other way. Pulling down the brim of my cap, hoping he won't see past the shades and the Bud cap, I get in line with him five people back. I stare at the floor when I board. He grabs a single seat and I pass him by, moving to the rear.

The Sheppard Avenue bus pulls out of the loop and into traffic. This bus route weaves through the Wilson Heights neighborhood until it hits Sheppard. Looking out the window at the houses and low-rises, I can see in my mind's eye the map Vinny customized, with all the red and green dots, old and new crimes clustered here in the Heights. Fires in empty houses, in Dumpsters and construction sites. Mutilated cats chained to telephone poles in the alleys. These are his own personal killing fields.

The overcast sky lends its gray color to these streets, making them look old and lifeless. I'm seeing things through the filter of his words in the diary, where everything tastes of death and decay. What happened to him when he was a kid—all the twisted things he only hints at, the events that made him—happened here.

Roach only rides three stops, six or seven blocks. He's not the only one getting off the bus, so I try and keep a couple of people between us in case he looks back. He steps out and turns left. I give him plenty of room. So close now, I don't want to spook him.

At the corner up ahead, he waits for the light to cross Faywood Boulevard. Scared he might look my way, I duck into a convenience store. Right on cue, two seconds later he glances down the sidewalk where I would have been. We're in a weird kind of synch—I'm reading his moves before he even makes them. This is what it must be like to be good at chess, able to see five moves ahead.

I let him get halfway across the intersection before

leaving the store. The light goes red, and I can't wait another minute for it to change again, so when he goes right on Cedar Road out of sight, I sprint across and almost get pancaked by a truck. At least the driver doesn't honk and attract attention to me.

It's a good thing I moved fast or I would have lost him. When I catch sight of him again he's climbing the stairs to a place on Cedar, third house in from the corner. Roach checks the mail, pulls out what looks like a magazine from the box and goes inside.

Cedar is a quiet tree-lined street, with houses a little worn around the edges.

Five minutes go by with me standing there, focused on the closed door. This is it. I've found the place. I do a walk-by, trying to keep my face forward while searching for any movement in the windows from the corner of my eye. The curtains are all drawn. Nothing to see except the number eighteen on the door. It's a short block, and when I get to the end I take a stroll around to the back alley to see the rear of the house.

Telephone poles run down the alley. I can't help wondering if he used any of them to hang up one of those cats. In a bizarre way, the neighborhood seems a little familiar, like I've already read the guidebook for it.

Number eighteen doesn't look much different from the rear, except for a couple of oil drums in the backyard. They could be for burning leaves. Or for storing a body. No, that's crazy! You don't dump a body in a drum in your backyard in the middle of summer. It would stink up the whole block. One of the drums has its top on, sealed shut. But that means nothing.

I'm getting a little shaky. Not thinking straight. I blink the sweat out of my eyes.

The back curtains are drawn. The windows of the basement, where Roach talked about being caged by his grandmother, are all painted black. Maybe he still keeps his room down there.

But is that all he's keeping down there? When he lost the diary he was still planning and preparing, but that was two weeks ago. He's had time to finally go over the edge and grab one of his targets. A woman to keep in *his* old cage.

Behind those blacked-out windows right now, he could be performing more of his experiments. But not on mice anymore.

I'm supposed to turn everything over to the cops now; that's what I promised Vinny. Give them the diary, the address. Lead them here and point him out.

But I don't know. Are they going to buy it? The diary is more of a scrapbook than a smoking gun. Would they even bring him in for questioning?

How long would it take to convince them this is real? I've already been down *that* road, and it went nowhere.

And is there any time left?

I pull off the Bud cap and run my hand through my sweaty hair.

God, I don't know. I just don't know.

I go down to the end of the alley. It leads back onto Faywood. Across the street on the corner there's a coffee shop. I walk over, just to be moving, to give me time to think. From inside the coffee shop I've got a good view of the front of number eighteen Cedar Road. I buy a brownie and go sit by the window. Jacob will be pissed if this thing eats up the rest of the day. But he always seems pissed. How will I know the difference?

Two bites into my brownie, Roach leaves his house wearing jeans and a T-shirt. He goes and waits at the bus stop across the street from me on Faywood. I shift seats so I'm hidden behind a cactus on the counter.

A minute later the bus comes. For a second I debate if I can still tail him without giving myself away. But I stay there, watching past the thorns of the cactus as he gets on.

I know what I told Vinny, but now that I'm here everything's different. I've got this idea. It's what Vin would call a seriously stupid idea.

The bus pulls away and I'm left staring at number eighteen over on Cedar.

I get up and go to the counter.

"Is there a pay phone?"

TWENTY-NINE

"Yeah," a bored voice answers on the fourth ring.

"Hey, Wayne. It's me. You doing anything?"

"Duncan. No. I'm doing nothing," he says. "And I plan on doing some more nothing later on."

"Remember what you were saying yesterday, about going straight?"

"I have been legal for twenty-four hours now. I think I'm cured."

"Well, how about starting your new legal life tomorrow? I need a little favor."

"An illegal favor?"

"What's illegal, anyway? Just someone else's rules, isn't that what you used to say?"

Part of me hates myself for doing this; it's like I'm waving a needle in front of an addict. Wayne's always been the devil on my shoulder—now I'm the devil on his. But I'm desperate. I need him.

"Legal is in the eye of the beholder," Wayne says. Beneath the joking I hear a sad edge to his voice. I try and block it out.

"I just need you to pick a lock. You can still do that, right?"

"The fingers never forget. What kind of lock?"

"I don't know."

"Well, what's the lock on?"

"A door. To a house."

He's quiet on the other end, and I'm holding my breath. He can't say no.

"Sounds like a B and E," Wayne says, serious now.

"It's not really a break and enter. Not for you. All you have to do is work the lock. Just get me in. For you, you're not going to be entering. And it's not really breaking either. You're just . . . opening."

"Right. Opening. So what, you're gonna rob some place?"

"I'm not going to take anything."

"Then why—"

"It would take too long, man. There's kind of a time crunch. I understand if you can't do it." It kills me to say that last part. I'm standing here at the phone in the coffee shop with my eyes squeezed shut, silently begging him to come do this for me.

After an eternity, Wayne says, "I can only do simple locks. No dead bolts."

"Okay."

"You need it done now?"

"Yeah."

"Where?"

THIRTY

Two double-chocolate brownies and thirty-five minutes later, Wayne shows up. It's started raining, and I'm waiting under the awning of the coffee shop. Spotting him across the street, I sprint over to him.

"It takes you half an hour to get here?" I say.

"You interrupted my nap," he tells me, using his hand to squeegee the rain from his bald head.

"Never mind, let's go." I'm impatient and jumpy from all the caffeine.

"Wait up. What's going on? What's the story?"

"Third house down on the side street there." I point it out. "I need to have a quick look inside."

"Why?"

Why will take forever to answer, so I give him the ultra-condensed version. "There's a guy who lives there who's a major psycho. He's planning to kill a woman. Don't ask how I know, but I do know this. He's gone right now, and I need to have a look around."

Wayne takes a moment, looking back and forth between

me and the house on Cedar. "You're screwing with me, right?"

"This is for real," I tell him. I guess there's something he sees in my eyes, desperation or determination, because he loses his doubting look.

"Is this what you've been doing with Vinny?"

"What do you mean?"

"You guys have been hanging out a lot, looking at maps and books and stuff. Then you shut up when I come around."

I underestimated Wayne, thinking he was too busy slacking and goofing off to notice anything was up.

"Me and Vinny have been trying to track this guy down," I say.

He uses his finger to flick some rain off his forehead. "What about me? You only bring me in when you need criminal help? Am I an idiot or something?"

"No. What are you talking about? It's just, everything's been happening so fast. And you've been working." What else can I say? True, I didn't think he'd be much help doing the heavy mental lifting. But there's no time now for hurt feelings or whatever. So I say, "Sorry, okay?"

He grumbles and shrugs. "Okay, I guess. But you owe me."

We start up Cedar. I take one last look down Faywood in the direction Roach left, but I don't see any buses coming. Both our shirts are wet now, and the storm's starting to kick it up a notch. I tell him how I saw Roach leave forty minutes ago. There's no way to know how much time we have.

In and out, I tell myself. This will be quick and painless.

"Anybody else live there?" he asks.

"Ahhh." I hadn't thought of that. The guy's a loner, but what about the grandmother? Is she still in the picture? "Yeah. There might be an old lady. His grandmother. I'm not positive."

Wayne takes the lead, climbing the stairs to Roach's house. He goes straight to the door and knocks loudly.

"What are you doing?" I ask.

"Knocking. I'm not going to give some old lady a heart attack." He sniffles and wipes his wet hands on his T-shirt. "Never do a house unless it's empty. You'll live longer."

We wait half a minute; then Wayne pounds harder. Another minute passes. No response.

"Okay, keep your eyes open," he tells me.

Reaching down, he pulls a pair of metal tools out of his sock. They look like instruments from a dentist's office. One's about five inches long, thin and bent at the tip. Wayne sticks it in, feels around, and wedges it into place. I study the houses across the street but don't see anybody watching. It's a sleepy little neighborhood where nothing ever happens. The second tool I recognize as something he made in metal shop, short with a blunt jag on the edge. This he uses more like a regular key, jiggling until it falls into place, then turning it clockwise.

The lock clicks and the door opens inward. Wayne disengages his tools, wipes the knob down with the end of his T-shirt, and motions me in.

I turn and say, "I'll take it from here." But he pushes me ahead and squeezes inside next to me.

"You don't have to—" I start to whisper.

"I know," he says, silencing me. "Make it quick."

It's a two-floor house, old and shabby. The carpets are worn; the paint shows some peeling on the ceiling. The smell of ammonia is in the air; someone's been cleaning. I move in, hyper-alert, my heart seizing up with every step. Around the corner at the end of the hall is a little kitchen/dining room with a table and two chairs. Across the hall from it there's a door with a padlock on it. The doorjamb is painted white, standing out against the older yellowy beige of the walls. Somebody did a repair job here.

This must be the door to *his* cage, the one he broke through years ago. The padlock is cold and heavy in my hand. I pull on it. Locked. He's got his own key to the cage now.

Wayne moves on past me, following the hall to what looks like the living room. I'm still studying the basement door when out of the corner of my eye, I catch him freezing suddenly. He shoots a look at me over his shoulder, then points into the living room and backs up a few steps.

Wayne flattens himself against the wall as I edge past him.

The TV is on. Sitting in an easy chair in front of it is a white-haired woman with her back to us. The grandmother.

Panic paralyzes me. My heart's beating so loud I'm sure she'll hear it. The TV's showing an episode of *Judge Judy*, only the volume is muted. A chill runs through my gut into my chest. She's the one who locked Roach up, the one he said has blood like acid. Seconds pass and nobody moves.

The crazy thought enters my head that she's dead, that he's killed and stuffed her, set her up like a mannequin in front of the TV. I'm about ready to bolt when she coughs. The sound is like a shock of electricity through me, and I can't help gasping.

I'm focused on the back of her head, expecting it to whip around any second and spot me.

Something flickers on her TV and my gaze shifts momentarily. I notice text scrolling at the bottom of the screen, large white words against a black background. It takes me a moment to realize it's the closed-captioning subtitles.

I move backward until I'm even with Wayne, leaning in close to whisper to him. "She's deaf."

His eyes are wide and the sweat is running freely down his face. He starts to retreat.

"This is too much," he breathes. "Even for me."

I can tell from the tremor in his voice that he's completely freaked. And there's nothing I want more right now than to make a run for it. But I can't. Not yet.

"Okay. Okay," I tell him. I stop by the basement door. "Just— I need you to open this lock."

He looks at me like I'm nuts and glances toward the living room.

"What?" he whispers. For a moment I think I've lost him.

Then he shakes his head. "Right. You watch her. If she twitches from that chair I'm gone."

I move over to the corner to keep an eye on her, and Wayne gets his tools back out.

A commercial comes on, but the grandmother makes no move to get up. From my vantage point all I can see of her is thinning white hair and the wrinkled gray skin of her neck. A deaf old lady watching TV. I'd almost feel guilty breaking in, but I know some of the things she did to that kid who became Roach.

"Come on," Wayne mutters, trying to work the lock with his sweaty hands.

A long minute stretches to the breaking point before I hear the click we're waiting for. Wayne looks over at me.

"Done," he says, and jams the tools in his pocket, wiping down the lock. "Now I'm gone, man."

I nod. "Okay."

"I'll wait for you out on the corner."

And he disappears down the hall without another word. Seconds later, I hear the door quietly open and shut.

I can barely breathe. There's no air in here.

Get a grip! Make it quick.

One last check on the grandmother, then I go to the door and pull the lock off the bracket. The door opens to darkness. Reaching in, I feel around on the walls for a switch. My fingers find it, and I send up a silent prayer.

A short staircase leads down to a low-ceilinged basement.

I take the lock with me, and after a moment's indecision I close the door behind me. In case Granny gets up. The air's cooler underground, and there's a stale chemical kind of smell. The stairs don't creak, thank God. Not that there's anybody to hear me.

Let's make this fast! I tell myself.

The low-wattage bulb in the ceiling casts the place in a dim gloom. Boxes are piled beside the stairs. A long wooden table is set against the wall, covered with papers and electrical equipment. A brighter light sits on top of a stack of books, shining on some kind of half-dissected speaker.

I peer around into the corner shadows, expecting—but dreading—to find something human there.

Nothing.

On the table stands a row of jars. That's where the smell is coming from. It's formaldehyde. Suspended in yellow liquid inside them are unidentifiable animal parts and whole corpses. Cats, small dogs, rodents—who knows? They're all drained of color. Tacked to the wall is a row of pictures that look like they've been torn from medical textbooks, showing anorexic women with protruding ribs, tight skin pulled over the bumps of their spine.

Near the jars, an empty Slurpee cup sits beside a few crumpled Mars bar wrappers.

I look up at the blackened windows. On the ledge are half a dozen cleaned rodent skulls.

What at first glance I assumed was some kind of radio turns out to be a police scanner. There's a list taped to it of different frequencies for different agencies: police, fire, paramedics.

On the tabletop there's a mess of papers, covered in the same scrawled handwriting I know from the diary. I dig through them a bit and find a set of photos.

Some are blurry, and some only catch half a face. But they're shots of women, obviously taken without their knowledge, in public places. He's stepped it up since the last entry in his diary. Gone from choosing targets to fully documenting them.

I've seen enough. There's nobody here. Time to go.

My foot is on the first stair when I catch sight of another door off in the corner of the basement. My eyes shift from that door to the stairs and the quick escape they promise.

I have to force myself to go over and look in the corner.

On either side of the doorjamb a metal bracket has been bolted into the wall. These brackets hold a four-foot, round metal bar that blocks the door. Better than a lock, this setup would keep a linebacker from breaking out. No doorknob. There's a rectangular hole cut in the wood at knee level, like a letter slot. Or an opening to shove a plate of food through.

God, no. Please no.

I crouch down and try and see through to the other side. But it's black in there and the dim light doesn't help.

I have to try and swallow a few times before I have enough spit to speak.

"Hello?" I say through the slot. "Somebody there?"

No sound from inside, not even breathing. But I don't know if I could hear anything past the blood pounding in my ears. I stand up.

"I—I'm going to open the door, okay?"

The bar has some heft to it. I lift it off the struts and hold it in one hand, resting the end on the floor. I use my other hand to pull the door open. There's no knob, so I have to stick my fingers in the letter slot to get a grip. I'm shaking, expecting something on the other side to grab me.

I swing the door open, jumping back.

Empty. Nothing but shadows. My head is pounding, nerves shivering, waiting for the shadows to move.

There's nothing but an empty plastic bucket on the cement floor. The space is clean but doesn't smell disinfected or anything. Looking at the inside of the door, I don't see any stains, no blood or splintering. It hasn't been used yet.

I let out a shivering breath. My sweaty T-shirt sticks to my back like a second skin.

Get out! Let's go.

Reaching out to shut the closet, I lift the bar to set it back in place. Then I hear a faint click come from the top of the stairs. I freeze with the bar in my hands. I'm in the corner, out of sight of the basement door above, but I can tell from the extra light spilling down that it's been opened.

I don't breathe. I don't blink. Twenty seconds pass before someone starts slowly down the stairs.

There's no time to move for cover under the staircase. I'm trapped in the corner like an insect. There's only one place left to hide. Stay in the open and I'm easy prey. As I move, my brain is screaming at me not to go in there. It's insane. But there's nowhere else.

So I slip inside the closet with the steel bar in my hand, pulling the door shut silently. The sudden dark almost pushes me over the edge, and it takes all the restraint I have in me to slow my breathing and keep quiet.

There's a faint shaft of light coming through the slot. Crouching on my knees, I peer out of the hole. The shadowed figure is halfway down. For a wild second I think it might be Wayne, coming back to get me. But the shadow's too tall. There's only one person it can be.

As he reaches the bottom of the stairs, I see him in the light. Roach's head swivels around, scanning the room. He walks around the staircase, giving the pile of boxes a wide berth in case someone's hiding there. In his right hand, I see the thin flash of a knife blade catching the light for an instant. When he's done looking at the boxes, he goes over to his table and examines his things. It was a mess when I got here, but it must have been his own particular mess because he reaches straight for the photos I uncovered. He knows they've been moved.

Roach turns with his back to the table and looks out over the basement, his head tilted up just a little, as if he's a rat tasting the air. Then his gaze settles on the closet door. And I'm dead.

I shift back so he won't see my eyes in the slot. But it's no good. He's moving toward me now. It takes forever for him to cover the space between the table and the door, like he's trying to catch a mouse and doesn't want to scare it off.

I rise, gripping the bar in my hands like a baseball bat. My palms are slick with sweat, but I'm clenching the steel like rigor mortis has set in.

The light filtering through the slot blacks out and I can feel him on the other side of the door. I press myself into the back of the closet and suck in a last breath.

There's only one way out, and that's through him.

Launching myself with all the momentum I can gain in this small space, I explode through the door right into him. Roach stumbles back a few feet into a shoulder-high pile of boxes. I'm thrown off balance and fall to one knee. While he steadies himself, I get up and back toward the stairs.

Roach moves to block me with his arms out at his sides, the knife in his right hand, six inches long and flashing a dull silver in the gloom. I tense up on the bar to try and keep him at bay. There's no way I can make a break for it up the stairs, because even halfway up he'd still be able to slash my legs out from under me.

Behind those thick lenses, his eyes study me with a cold curiosity. In the dim light his pupils look huge, the size of dimes, taking over the color of his eyes as if they're sucking in all available light to see me better. He twitches his knife hand and I flinch a half step to the side. Easy to see who's in control here. He gets closer without even seeming to move his feet.

I edge away. In my peripheral vision I can sense the table behind me. I'm running out of room.

Roach moves into the light spilling from the hallway above, becoming a silhouette, the featureless shadow from my nightmares. My knees feel watery, like they're going to betray me and fold. I take one more step back, and my foot lands on some paper fallen on the floor. I lose my footing and my butt hits the table hard.

He lunges at me, a shadowy blur, and I kick out, leaning my weight on the tabletop. I only graze him, but enough to change the angle of the slashing knife. He falls into me and I slip away before he can grab hold.

Raw panic flows through me, the pulse of adrenaline making everything louder and brighter.

Swinging the bar with everything I've got, I catch him in the shoulder. He grunts, and I haul back and whack him in the ribs. I pull back again for another swing, but he leaps away from the table and slashes out, cutting a line of fire into my left forearm. I let out a strangled gasp and drop the bar. The steel hits the cement floor with a loud clang.

As I stagger back I see he's half bent over, one arm shielding his side. The back of my ankle connects with the bottom stair, and before he can move or I can think, I swing around and scramble up the stairs. I take them three at a time, feeling the phantom pain of his knife cutting into my legs.

At the top of the stairs I sense him right behind me. I

explode into the hallway, bouncing off the wall and racing around the corner for the front door. I yank frantically at the doorknob until my fear-blinded brain remembers to flick the lock. It pops and I throw the door open, hearing a yell of animal rage behind me.

But I'm outside on the porch before he can catch up, and I leap the four stairs to the ground, crashing to my knees. Cutting across the lawn, I bolt down Cedar Road, my feet moving faster than my brain can register. The rain is falling hard now, slicking the sidewalk. I don't even think of glancing back until I hit Wilson Heights Boulevard. Pausing at the corner, I catch sight of the blood pouring out of me, so much of it that even the heavy rain isn't watering it down as it runs off my fingertips. I'm barely even feeling it. It's like somebody else's arm. Stunned by the sight of the open gash in me, I look up to see Roach coming on fast, twenty feet away.

I break into a run, sprinting down the block, confused about where to go, which direction will give me an escape.

Don't look back! I tell myself. Don't look!

Two blocks later my lungs are burning. I'm way out of shape.

Where's Wayne? The question flickers through my brain, but there's no time to think. It's just me and Roach now.

There's a momentary break in traffic, so I cut across the street, trying anything to shake him. Before I get to the other curb I hit a pothole puddle and roll my ankle. The pain shoots up my right leg, cutting through the shock and adren-

aline. I do a couple of hop steps onto the sidewalk, quickly testing it out. My ankle's screwed. I lean on the chain-link fence that runs beside the sidewalk, twisting to see where he is now.

Directly across the boulevard, Roach has stopped, his head whipping left and right as he scans for an opening in traffic. I don't see the knife in his hands, but I'm sure he's got it.

Blinking the rain out of my eyes and pulling myself along the chain links, I look to see what's on the other side of the fence.

It's the subway line. Must be the stretch from Wilson to Downsview. Wilson Station can't be more than a block away. I'm so close.

Screw the ankle! It can hurt later.

I start a staggering jog down the sidewalk. After half a block I hear wheels screeching on wet pavement behind me, then horns and shouting.

"Nut!" "Look where you're going!" "Get out of the road!" voices are yelling back there.

No time to look. I hit Wilson Street, stumbling across the intersection on a yellow light. People back away from me. I'm bleeding and soaked to the bone. Nothing matters but making the next train.

I'm wheezing like an asthmatic when I get to the subway entrance. If I can just catch the train, I'm free. I'm gone. Game over.

I take the stairs at full speed, hanging on the railing, half hopping, half sliding down. Approaching the ticket booth, I consider jumping the turnstile, but I really don't think I could clear it. So I spend precious seconds scrambling to flash my transit pass. By the wide-eyed stare of the woman in the booth, I can tell I must look insane—running and gasping, covered in blood.

I limp straight to the southbound platform, sliding along the wall to keep myself vertical. The pain in my ankle is dull compared to the agony of the burning gash in my arm, finally breaking through to my shocked brain. Don't know how much blood I've lost, but it's still flowing. I watch it drop on the dirty green tiles. The slightest of breezes blows past, the stirring of a train in the tunnel. I walk over to the edge and see the white headlights in the dark.

"Come on," I plead with it. "Come on."

As I'm staring into the black of the tunnel, out of the corner of my eye I see someone step out onto the platform. My eyes shift slowly over to him.

Roach walks casually toward me, like he only wants to ask me the time. He knows there's nowhere left to run. Roach is winded, his acne-scarred face deep red. Hunched a little to his left, he keeps his arm at his side, protecting himself. I must have cracked a few ribs with the bar.

Letting him come closer, staring into those dark buggy eyes, I try to time it just right. Then I fake with my crippled left hand and throw a hook with my right. He sees it coming like I'm in slow motion, dodging it easily. I stagger with the momentum of the missed punch, and before I can balance again, Roach hits me with a body check.

I stumble and fall off the edge of the platform, hitting the tracks hard and knocking what little wind I had left out of me. My eyes refuse to focus. All I see is two blurry white eyes coming toward me. There's a rumbling sound that seems to come at me from all directions. The tracks vibrate under my back, and my last active brain cells tell me that those aren't eyes I'm seeing, shining from the dark.

Get up! Now!

Pushing myself up on my elbows is a major effort, but I get from my elbows to my knees, and finally, shaking, to my feet. Reaching up to the platform, I set my palms flat on the tiles and get ready for one final exertion.

My unfocused eyes pick out a pair of shoes in front of my hands. Stunned and stupid, I follow them up to the shadow standing above.

The rumble of the train turns to thunder.

One of the shoes kicks me in the face; not hard, just enough to push me away. I lunge back to the platform, reaching to pull myself up. His foot shoots out again, but I catch it this time. He tries to shake me. But I know the only way out is through him. So I put my weight into it and give his foot a yank. It's enough. He gives way and falls past me onto the tracks.

The air splits open with a blast from the train's horn. Thirty feet away. No time to climb out even if I still had the strength.

I crouch and roll under the platform's slight overhang, trying to squeeze myself into the thin wedge of space there. I flatten myself into the stone.

The last thing I see is Roach staggering to a standing position, his glasses gone, holding his hands out blindly. He moves to try and escape to the northbound tracks. Then there's the scream of metal on metal as the train brakes. Sparks fly, and my scream joins the train's. I think I hear other voices screaming too, from above.

Impact. Blinding pain. The world goes black, and I'm falling a very long way, getting smaller and smaller, carrying our screams down with me.

Then nothing.

THIRTY-ONE

SUBWAY ASSAULT ENDS IN DEATH

Police are investigating the death of a man hit by a train at Wilson subway station. In what may have been a failed mugging, two males were seen fighting on the southbound platform when one man fell to the tracks as a train was approaching the station. Witnesses report that in the ensuing struggle, as the fallen man tried to climb back onto the platform, the other male also fell to the tracks and into the path of the oncoming train.

The train was unable to brake in time. One male died on the scene from massive injuries. The other is presently in critical condition at Baycrest Hospital. Names are being withheld pending notification of next of kin.

THIRTY-TWO

The guy in the mirror could have escaped from the morgue. Pressing down on the sink, I lean in for a closer inspection. My right eye has no white in it; the brown iris is surrounded by red. It's what the doctors call a subconjunctival hemorrhage. Doesn't look real, more like a special effect. They say it's a minor condition that will clear up in a week or two.

"Okay in there?"

That's Mom. This is my first solo trip to the toilet. She's been helping me with sitting and standing, steadying me and looking the other way when I tell her to. I was thinking the nurses could handle those duties, but she insisted. I'm back to being her baby again. I think she likes it that way.

"I'm good," I call through the door.

The light's too bright in here, making my stitches appear even more gruesome. They sewed me up with fifteen stitches, running from behind my ear down the back of my neck. Another twenty on my arm—they had to do both deep sutures *and* surface ones to close it up. There might be some nerve damage. Got to wait and see. My other arm is shot too, with a mid-forearm break and two screws in there to heal it straight.

What else? A minor concussion and some serious road rash where I got dragged along under the platform.

I look like crap. But you should see the other guy.

Roach, aka Scott Weber, was pulped, crushed, and left without any real features to identify him. Good thing he had his health insurance card in his wallet.

The cops came and went, and came and went. There was some confusion about the sequence of events. People had spotted me being chased into the station. If it was a botched mugging, why had Weber followed me like that, into a public place?

"Sorry, I can't remember," I told them. "He tried to rob me. He had a knife. But it's all really hazy."

The concussion bailed me out, gave me an excuse to be vague and confused. There were enough people who saw Roach chasing me—and the security video showing him attacking me on the platform—to fill in most of the blanks. And he still had the knife on him that sliced my arm open.

It came out on the news that there had been a prior assault charge against Scott Weber. A prostitute had been beaten up, but the charge was dropped when the woman refused to testify. So even if the cops still had some questions, it was clear Weber wasn't exactly a model citizen.

When I come out of the washroom, Mom's right outside the door.

"Did you manage?" she asks.

"Yes, Mum. I'm a *big* boy now."

I try a smile that turns into a wince when it stretches my stitches.

Dad gets up from his seat by the window. He's not looking so hot himself, staying here during the day and working the graveyard every night. If Mom's my nurse, Dad's my guard. Death almost got me, but he'll be here to scare it off next time.

"Go home, Dad," I tell him. "You've got to be at work again in like six hours."

I walk over to the bed, and they follow me on either side, ready to lift and carry me, burp me and change my diaper.

"Thanks, guys. I think I can make it."

I sit down on the edge of the bed.

"Do you want some ice water?" Mom asks. "Or some Jell-O?"

I shake my head slowly, wincing at even that small movement.

"Watch some TV," Dad suggests.

"No. No. You guys should take a break. I'm not going anywhere. It'll be a couple more days before they let me go home."

Dad lets loose with a monster yawn.

"Go," I say to him. "Get some sleep."

There's a knock at the door, and Wayne pokes his head in. "You're not getting your sponge bath or anything indecent, are you?"

"I wish," I say.

"Sir. Ma'am." Wayne greets the folks.

"Wayne," Dad grunts, not thrilled to see him.

"Well, maybe we will take a breather," Mom says, sensing the sudden chill in the air.

Before they leave, Mom comes over and combs my hair with her fingers, studying my face. "I really don't like the looks of that eye."

"Like the doctor said, it'll be gone in a couple weeks—the redness, not the eye," I tell her. "It's like a hickey."

"Hmmm," she says, trying on a weak smile. "I'll be back first thing in the morning."

"Okay."

"Night, kid," Dad says.

When they're gone, I have to deal with Wayne screwing around with the controls on my bed.

"Let me give it a spin," he says, hopping on with his dirty shoes and ratty jean jacket. "So what's with the folks? I get the feeling they've got a voodoo doll of me at home and they're going to rush back to the Jungle to hammer nails into it."

"You're the devil on my shoulder, man. Darth to my Luke."

"Right. What a load. You're the one who talked me into a felony."

Wayne gets tired of the contorting bed and flicks on the TV. Him and Vinny have been coming by every day. We're the only ones who know what really happened. And we're going to keep it that way. Taking it to the grave.

"The cops been back?" he asks.

"Yeah."

"And?"

"And nothing. I have a concussion. I can't remember. I'm confused. Where am I? What's my name?"

Wayne nods. "Massive head injury. Good excuse." He scratches his stubbly scalp. "I never should have left you alone there."

After Wayne took off that day, he went and waited on the corner. But he was getting drenched, so he ran over to the coffee shop to get out of the rain. He didn't see Roach coming home. Wayne said he was drying himself off with a wad of napkins when he looked out the window and saw me being chased. I was already two blocks away by then, and running hard. He tried to follow but lost sight of me. He was still searching when he heard the sirens converging on Wilson Station.

Wayne actually saw me being loaded into the back of the ambulance. He couldn't call my parents or talk to the cops without giving everything away. I mean, we had just committed a felony. So he went to the hospital and found out I was still breathing. He came real close to running into my mother when she got there, but managed to slip away unseen.

"Hey, don't let it eat you up," I tell him. "All's well that ends . . . in death and disfigurement."

I lean back on the bed beside Wayne. He stops flicking channels when he finds a rap video.

I reach over to my bedside table and take a sip of warm

water, using a straw. "Remember when you were talking about going straight? No more scamming?"

"Doesn't sound like me."

"Seriously."

Wayne sighs. "Yeah. I remember."

"I guess I kind of wrecked that for you." I take the straw from my water and use it to scratch an itch under my cast, careful to avoid the stitches. "What do you say we make a deal," I say, "and stay legal from now on?"

Wayne reaches in the side pockets of his jacket.

"Tell you what," he says. "Let's sign that deal in pudding."

He pulls out two sealed cups of chocolate pudding. "I lifted these from somebody's lunch tray."

"Oh, man." I shake my head, groaning.

"The deal is . . . ," Wayne tells me, peeling back the lid and dipping his finger in. "When the pudding's done"—he pauses to lick his finger clean—"so are our lives of crime."

He hands me the other pudding. He's quit too many times for me to really buy it. Like he says—whether he's working a lock, doing some lifting, or taking a commission—"The fingers never forget." But right now those fingers are smeared with chocolate, and I really want to believe him.

So I say, "Deal."

I don't know what it is that pulls me out of a dead sleep. It's not a sound, or a change in the light. The blinds are still drawn, and the hospital room is pleasantly dim. I sniff the air.

A smell. That's what it is. A smell so familiar . . .

"So you're still breathing, eh?" she says.

I glance over to the source of the voice. Kim's sitting in a chair she's pulled up beside my bed.

I'm real groggy. My head feels like it's stuffed with cotton balls. I give her a lazy smile, breathing in her vanilla scent. "You smell like ice cream."

"You always say that," she tells me, her voice with a touch of sadness.

"Makes me hungry."

She's quiet for a while, studying the wreckage of my face. I'm still smiling, in a dopey kind of way. It's a real effort to keep my eyes open. I'm so impossibly happy to see her. My phantom girlfriend, sitting there in the flesh.

Kim shakes her head. "You look like roadkill."

"Yeah. But you should see the other guy."

"They said it was a mugging. That you fought back."

"Didn't want to lose my library card." I laugh softly at my own joke.

She sighs. "I'd whack you on the side of the head if you didn't already have a concussion."

"I'd settle for a spanking." I try to waggle my eyebrows, but it hurts too much. "You mad at me or something?"

"Yes. No." Kim reaches up and ruffles her short blond hair, giving me a growl of frustration. "You were always so busy trying to rescue me from my life. Remind me now, who's the one who needs protection?"

I'm finding it hard to focus on her words. She sounds

mad, but it's a good mad. She doesn't hate me or anything. She's just worried. Everybody's always worried about me.

"Miss you," I say.

"I know."

I almost doze off then, but use all my strength to keep my eyes on her. In the dimness, Kim's a long blond shadow stretched out on the chair.

We're quiet for a little while. Then she gets up. I raise my head.

"Don't go," I say.

"Sleep," she tells me.

"But—"

"Go to sleep."

I want to fight it, but my head suddenly feels a hundred pounds heavier, sinking down into a pillow soft as melting ice cream.

The lights go out in my brain and I give up, letting sleep pull me under.

Way later, I wake up with the faint memory of someone being in the room with me. I can't remember who, until I pick up the scent she left behind.

My vanilla phantom.

THIRTY-THREE

The stitches came out after two weeks. The cast stays on for six to eight.

After fourteen days of rest under Mom's surveillance, I get a little twitchy and decide to go back to work. I'm actually shocked I still have a job. I thought Jacob would have ratted me out when I took off for lunch that day and never came back. Maybe he never even noticed.

When he sees me with my cast, walking in the door of the lost and found, he says: "A lot of good you'll be now. One arm and a limp."

Love you too, you old fart.

Back in the stacks, my lawn chair is still here. Same chair, same dust, same fossilized Post-its swept under the shelves. Nothing changes down in the morgue.

The cops stopped bugging me weeks ago. I was worried at first they might go searching Roach's place and find my blood in the basement, my fingerprints on that steel bar. Talking to the cops, I found out more from them than they got from me. My story didn't change—I couldn't remember.

But they let slip about Weber living with his grandmother, and how she was being very uncooperative.

I guess they had no real reason to press it, no reason to get a search warrant or anything. The investigation was closed. Case cleared.

And nobody will ever know. Except me, Wayne, and Vinny.

On the weekend we had a big barbecue out in back of the Jungle. Guess what I used to start up the fire. I doused the pages from the diary with lighter fluid and stood there with Vin and Wayne, watching them burn.

I've been thinking about the grandmother, that deaf old lady who caged her grandson. What would she do when she discovered what he had been up to in the basement?

I can only see her through his eyes, his words. So I think she'd just take what she found as proof that her grandson was what she'd always suspected. She'd mop up the blood and throw away his things. "Very uncooperative" they called her. From what I read she sounds half nuts herself. It doesn't really matter now, anyway. All Roach's plans died with him.

I settle into my chair and ease my foot up to rest on a shelf.

Kim called yesterday. It could have been a pity call, checking up on the poor broken-down ex. But she did call. That's got to mean something, right?

She's playing in the Toronto summer league, so I'm going to catch one of her games this week. And see what happens.

Jacob rings the bell. We reunite a woman with her bowling ball. I grab a cup of water at the cooler and pop a painkiller.

"You made all the papers," Jacob says, not looking up from his word jumble.

I swallow. "Five weeks of pain for fifteen minutes of fame."

He circles a word with his pen. "So why'd you come back?"

I lean my cast on the cooler's jug. Good question. I don't need the money that bad. But escaping the oven of my apartment for the cooler air underground, that's a real incentive.

"Don't know," I say. "What would you do without me?"

"Get some peace and quiet."

I shrug, saying, "You can get that when you're dead."

My words hang in the air a long time, like stones I've tossed into the bottomless pit of Jacob. I wait for a sign that they've hit something. He focuses on the blank wall straight ahead. Hard to say what thoughts are passing behind those eyes. Jacob would make a great statue.

Why I try, I don't know.

But then—

"Guess so," he mumbles, so low I almost miss it.

I'm stunned. This is the closest we've ever been to actually having a conversation.

I think of saying something more. But I leave it at that, with my small victory. He heard me. And for once he didn't brush me off.

Walking into the stacks, I take my post and lean back. The morgue is quiet today. Like every day. We've both been doing our time down here. My sentence is almost up. Jacob might just be a lifer.

But I've still got a couple more weeks to work on him.

THIRTY-FOUR

"What are we doing here?" Vinny asks. "I thought we were going for Slurpees."

We're standing at the fence that surrounds the pool in Amesbury Park. It's after midnight, and the crickets are rioting in the grass, filling the air with an electric buzz.

"Later. Let's go for a dip. I'm dying in this heat," I say. "If I don't get some relief I'm going to spontaneously combust."

"Man, that's a myth. People don't just burst into flames."

"Wait a couple minutes and I'll make a believer out of you."

These are the dog days of August, when the air is so still that the air you breathe out is the air you breathe back in again.

"Go ahead. But make it quick," Vin says.

"You're coming with me."

"You know I don't swim."

"You don't swim when people are staring at you. Ain't nobody here but you and me, and I can barely see you."

All I can make out are shadows around us. There's only a flicker of street light that makes it through the trees, reflecting off the pool. In the dark, the only thing that stands out is my cast. It's so white it seems to glow.

Vinny looks at the fence, looks at me. "Just how hard did you get hit in the head?"

"Hard enough," I say.

"Anyway, I can't climb that."

The fence is eight feet high, the links at the top bent over from years of late-night trespassers.

"If I can climb it with one arm, you can too," I tell him.

It's a struggle, and it isn't pretty with my useless left arm, but I manage to make it up and over. My right arm is pretty much back to normal, but the long red scar throbs and itches sometimes. I drop the last few feet to the pool deck by the deep end, wincing at the way the impact makes my head pound. The migraines have died down, but I still get the occasional flare-up.

"Nice dismount," Vin says.

I kick off my shoes and slip off my socks. "Let's see you try."

He takes a minute to plan his climb before he starts, making calculations in that massive brain of his. His dismount is smoother, just to show me up.

"I don't know, man," he says. "I didn't bring a swimsuit."

I test the water temperature with my toes. "Warm but sweet."

"You going to swim in your jeans?" he asks.

I drop my pants in response, then throw off my T-shirt.

"You strip naked and I'm out of here," he says.

"I'll keep my briefs on," I assure him. "Don't want to make you feel inadequate."

"What about your cast?"

From my pants pocket I pull out a plastic Safeway bag and some elastic bands. "Be prepared. That's the Boy Scout motto."

"Really? I thought it was 'You gotta fight for your right to party.'"

"No, that was the Beastie Boy scout motto."

I stick my left arm in the bag and fix the bands really tight, for a waterproof seal. Meanwhile, Vinny strips down to his underwear and a long-sleeved sweatshirt.

"You try and swim in that and you'll sink like a rock," I tell him.

"Look the other way. I don't need an audience."

I leave him to his slow striptease, stepping up to the edge and jumping into the deep end. In daylight, the water is a bright chlorine blue. But in the dark, the water changes to a deeper blue, mirroring the night sky.

I told Vin a half-lie back there when I said I was here to get some heat relief. I *was* feeling combustible, but the real reason I'm here lies down at the bottom of the pool.

The cast makes me awkward. I can only stroke with my right arm. I move out into the middle of the deep end. Taking a deep breath, I dive.

Weeks ago, on the scorching day I was here with Wayne,

the darkness that came over me underwater was all in my head. Now the dark is real. It's so black, it leaves me blind. I push down, stroking deeper, until my hands touch bottom. Then I just hang there, waiting. My eyes are wide but useless.

After almost a minute, my lungs start to protest.

I wait for them. For the screams I've been hearing, awake and asleep, this last year, echoing inside my head. I hang still, weightless.

But it's so quiet right now, like the whole world has stopped between breaths. My lungs start to burn. I sweep my arms out over the bottom, searching for contact, terrified of finding it. But there's nothing. Only empty water and silence.

My lungs are starving. Can't hold out any longer.

I whisper a silent *Sorry*. Then I kick off for the surface.

She's not here anymore. Her screams have faded away to nothing. I guess even echoes have to die sometime.

Breaking through, I suck in the night air. By the side of the deep end, Vinny's hanging on to the ladder with his chin just above the surface. I stroke over to him.

My oldest memory is a blurry one, of dog-paddling in shallow water, breathing the smell of chlorine. It must be from those baby swims Mom took me on before I could even walk. Sometimes when the water's warm, like now, I can't even tell where my skin ends and the water begins. I was born to swim.

"Man," Vinny says when I grab hold of the ladder beside

him. "You were down there so long I thought you were never coming up again."

Quietly, I say, "She's not there."

"Who's not where?"

"You know, the girl. Maya. She's not down there anymore."

Vinny gives me a worried look, but then he nods. "That's good, man. Let her sleep."

"Yeah."

I look out over the calm dark water and whisper, " 'Night."

ABOUT THE AUTHOR

Graham McNamee. Male Caucasian. 5'10". Brown hair. Brown eyes. Do not approach. Extremely shy. Author of: *Hate You, Nothing Wrong with a Three-Legged Dog,* and *Sparks. Hate You* was an ALA Best Book for Young Adults and an ALA Quick Pick, won the Austrian Children's Book Award, and was nominated for the Governor General's Award. *Sparks* won the PEN/Phyllis Naylor Working Writer Fellowship.

Born and raised in Toronto, McNamee has been sighted in Vancouver. Present whereabouts unknown.